CW01508755

FAN SERVICE

SAMANTHA ANN

Edited by PROOF POSITIVE
Cover by KIM CAVRAK
Formatted by GARNET CHRISTIE

To the 'good girls' who enjoy being punished every now and again.

HANGUL CHEAT SHEET

Consonants:	Vowels:
ㄱ – g,k	ㅏ – ah
ㄴ – n	ㅐ – ay
ㄷ – d	ㅑ – ya
ㄹ – r,l (say "real" but with an l in the beginning "leal")	ㅒ – yae
ㅁ – m	ㅓ – eo
ㅂ – b	ㅔ – eh
ㅅ – s	ㅕ – yeo
ㅇ – no sound if it starts the word. 'ng' sound if it finishes	ㅗ – o
ㅈ – j	ㅘ – wa
ㅊ – ch	ㅙ – wae
ㅋ – k	ㅚ – oe
ㅌ – t	ㅛ – yo
ㅍ – p	ㅜ – u
ㅎ – h	ㅝ – whoa
ㄲ – gg	ㅞ – we
ㄸ – dd	ㅟ – wi
ㅃ – bb	ㅠ – yu
ㅉ – jj	ㅡ – oo
ㅆ – ss	ㅢ – ui
	ㅣ - ee
	ㅖ -ye

FAN SERVICE OST

Your Gravity – UP10TION
    Beautiful MAZE – DRIPPIN
    FIRST – EVERGLOW
    INVITATION (Feat. Goeko)- JUNNY, Gaeko
    LIKE THAT – BABYMONSTER
    Lovers In The Night – Seori
    EOEO – UNIQ
    text me – YOU DAYEON
    Sketch – dori
    Keep me up – B.I
    Like a Movie – B1A4
    Officially Cool – BANG YEDAM, WINTER

CHAPTER ONE

S ophia stood in front of the full-length mirror in her bedroom, phone held up to show her bestie, Bridgette, the fifth outfit she had attempted to put together for the CLAR1T concert the next night.

"You are not wearing *that* to the concert!" Bridgette scolded on FaceTime, rolling her eyes at another outfit.

"Why not? It's cute and comfy," Sophia argued as she gave a little turn to get a view of her butt in the black skinny jeans. The simple white t-shirt with a colorful graphic gave the outfit a slight pop of color, and her combat boots made for a comfy and pleasing concert outfit. "If I throw a leather biker jacket over—"

"No!" Bridgette screamed, silencing Sophia. "You have VVIP tickets; you'll get to meet CLAR1T after the show, and you're telling me *that's* what you want to wear?"

"You act like me wearing something out of this world would somehow change the fact that close to two hundred people will be lined up to simply wave and high-five these boys. Not to mention they've already seen four hundred people at their previous stops." Sophia rolled her eyes as she plopped down on her bed, feeling defeated from another failed outfit choice. "They're barely going to perceive me between the other thousands of fans they've interacted with."

And Sophia wanted to keep it that way. She had never been one to try to stand out in the crowd. She was an average woman, with an average job, and an average life. And she liked that. Her only out-of-the-ordinary decision was applying for an English teaching job in Korea. A job submission she was still waiting to hear back from before she told anyone she had applied.

"So by your logic, you should count yourself out without even trying?" Bridgette bit back. "Soph, you're one of those two hundred fans lucky enough to nab VVIP for a stop on CLARIT's first ever US tour. A tour that sold out in under ten minutes, I might add."

"And?" Sophia knew a Bridgette pep talk was coming.

"Beesh, you have luck on your side! Your probability of catching their eyes went up exponentially when you got those tickets. And on top of that, you are a freaking hottie!" Bridgette winked.

"You're ridiculous." Sophia blushed at her friend's hyping up. Bridgette could get Sophia to take tiny steps out of her comfort zone with her pep talks.

That's probably why her late-night study café had become a large success in their city. Bridgette would hand people their coffee and pastry with some added words of encouragement, and customers would be invigorated, not only by the caffeine and sugar, but by Bridgette's inspirational commentary.

"You're gonna wear that tight black skirt you wore at my b-day party, that red velvet bralette I saw you add to your cart during one of our shopping sprees, and that black mesh bodysuit with the embroidered birds or flowers or whatever on it that you bought to wear for a man who was undeserving of it." Bridgette had picked out an entire outfit from memory. Her mind was seriously scary sometimes. But it clicked for Sophia why Bridgette never needed to write down a customer's order at the café.

"I can't wear that in public!" Sophia grumbled, turning to her closet and looking at the drawer that hid the lingerie in question.

"You can and you will. You got hot-ass curves, show 'em off." Bridgette continued her hype until they both heard jingling bells, meaning someone had walked into Bridgette's shop. "I gotta go, but send me a pic of the outfit I just put together. I wanna see before you go to the show."

The video disappeared and "call ended" lit up the phone.

Sophia exhaled, falling back onto her bed, knowing that if she didn't send the picture to Bridgette, the woman would just show up at her door the next morning before she left for work. Perks of living in the apartment building next door to your best friend.

She sat up, grabbing all Bridgette's suggested pieces from the closet and tossed them on. She didn't want to admit that Bridgette was right, Sophia looked good. Better than good. She looked hot. Snapping the photo and sending it off, it wasn't even a minute before several expletives and praise were thrown her way from Bridgette.

She laughed at her hype woman as she changed back into her sweats, agreeing to the outfit choice and climbing into bed for the night.

She decided to scroll through the pictures and videos of the concerts from the last CLAR1T stop on Twitter, along with all the fan projects that were being set for her local shows. Amid the high-quality photos, the merch unboxings, and the fan stories from the shows, a very random tweet caught her attention.

@user16583: If you're going to a CLAR1T show and have the VVIP hi-touch, show them an upside-down V. You won't be disappointed.

She clicked on the account to see if there was more information, but there was nothing. Not even a profile picture or bio. They had no followers and followed no one. There was only that one tweet. A tweet with no likes or retweets, and yet it showed up on her search page when she looked up CLAR1T. How it popped into her feed was beyond her, but she chose to ignore it and continue scrolling to see pictures of her favorite six boys.

As she watched some of the fan service the members were giving to so many fans during the show, she gave a heavy sigh. Why should she think that she could be someone else?

I'm no different than any of these other fans.

She glanced at the outfit Bridgette had chosen, and for some reason she felt a glimmer of hope that maybe her best friend would be right and she could make at least one of the members do a double take. She let her delusion lull her to sleep.

Maybe...

CHAPTER TWO

성준was mentally exhausted. He didn't want to wave at fans for an extra two hours after the show they'd just put on. Even though it felt like one of his best performances of the last few months.

He loved performing. When he was on stage, he was in his element. It was like he had a split personality. Not as drastic as Jaehyeong, but he loved to perform and to make people excited about CLAR1T's music. But the second he was off the stage, he wanted nothing to do with all the extras necessary to maintain his image for the sake of the company and the fame. He didn't want to interact with people. He just wanted to be in his hotel room, laid out on his bed.

Maybe that bed had another person in it—that all depended on how horny he was. The fact that the other guys in the group didn't seem interested in the many possibilities of their touring surprised him. Sure, 지훈 used his secret word first, to the shock of all of them, but instead of enjoying her and moving on, he was sulking because she had rejected his offer of a relationship. After one night he had fallen in love with a girl?!

A relationship? On tour? 미쳤다! This was the time to relish

being single and enjoy a different person at every stop. In LA, 성준 was so jetlagged he couldn't even stay awake long after the shows to savor his free time. He needed something at this stop or he would most likely go mad. A nice, warm, consenting adult to take out his sexual frustration. A person to bury his dick deep inside for another form of euphoric release he couldn't get while on stage.

That's why he'd sent the tweet last night. His burner account. He only used it to scroll through what fans were saying about the group, but something came over him and he typed up that tweet. The odds of anyone seeing it were slim to none. He had no followers, no profile, no photo. But he thought, in the off chance someone would see it, that person would be his for the night. If it worked that night, he would post it for every show on tour.

What fan wouldn't want one mind-blowing night with an idol? He had read some of the scenarios fans created putting themselves into wild concepts and crazy encounters, so why not give a few lucky fans the chance to actually experience that?

He had heard stories from the older idol groups in the company of how some fans would slip notes with phone numbers or hotel keys. One said he was even handed a condom with the girl's number. Idols had their systems of getting around the rules, and they passed them down from generation to generation, adding more stealth. As technology got smarter, their rule breaking had to as well.

But after a whole day, his message had received no responses, not one like. Hell, there wasn't even a reply asking what he meant. And so he had resigned himself to the idea that no one had seen his message, and he would have to sneak out that night to find someone in a bar or something.

He wiped the sweat off his body before throwing the branded tour long-sleeve on and following the rest of the members to go back out and greet the group of fans who were able to get up close and personal, even if for only a few seconds.

"준비됐음?" Woo Shin asked through a heavy sigh. He wanted to be there even less than 성준. *Poor guy has too much going on in his head. If someone needs to get some relief…it's him.*

성준 gave a nod and wrapped his arm around Woo Shin's neck,

pulling him close to rub his knuckles across the top of the sweat-covered hair of his friend and groupmate.

"집어쳐." Woo Shin pushed 성준 off, and while his tone was annoyed, a small smirk crept across his lips, which meant he secretly enjoyed the brotherly love they shared.

One of the new tour managers ran over to them to have them follow her down the hall, back into the much emptier theater. Jaehyeong bounced beside her, trying his best attempt at small talk, making the rest of the boys laugh at how obvious he was that he liked her.

When she opened the doors and they walked back onto the stage, the screams of two hundred fans still sounded like the thousand or so who had been in there only a few minutes ago. He had to hold back his flinch from the piercing cries. He didn't think he would ever get used to the initial shock of those screams.

The line started funneling past them, where the members waved, sent finger hearts, blew kisses, and even high-fived and shook fans' hands. He joined in, giving the fan service that was required of him and even playing up the bromance of the group. He could play his part well.

Finally, he could see the finish line. There were only about twenty fans left in the line. Once they were out, he could leave and find some fun he was in desperate need of. He could tell that his hand wouldn't cut it that night. He let out a sigh as he realized his tweet had failed and probably wasn't going to be useful at any of the other shows either.

As they neared the end, he continued giving finger hearts blindly when he caught something in his peripheral. A downward V. Two fingers pointed down to the ground, and the symbol was making its way toward him.

His eyes moved quickly from the hand, up the arm, to a curvy figure he always appreciated and a revealing top that had some stitched roses and other flowers barely hiding an insanely gorgeous pair of breasts. Holy fuck, he wanted to bury his face in between them sucking and biting them. He took in her short tight black skirt that held thick thighs he was already pleading internally to be crushed between. His hands made tight fists as he thought of how much he wanted to grab those hips of hers as she bounced on his cock. He wanted to lean over to get a better view of her ass but it would be too obvious, and instead, as she approached, he matched her downward V and looked to one of the security guards.

He had instructed them that if he were to ever throw that sign, they needed to escort the fan out and to the small greenroom as a matter of safety. He had rules to follow when it came to being seen with people of the opposite sex, but he also knew how to break them. As did the other members.

When she finally reached him, his eyes went to her face, where he was rendered incapable of any form of thought or speech. The combination of her choppy bob of soft-looking, coppery light-brown hair and her eyes, a brilliant shade of green, captivated him. And her lips. Fuck, her lips. Plump, deep maroon, and shimmery with gloss—perfect for wrapping around his cock. The thoughts of smearing that gloss over her face and his dick had him pulling the front of his shirt down to cover his pants. Sweatpants were not a smart choice.

He knew he was horny and wanted a good fuck, but he hadn't imagined that feeling the primal need to be near a person, inside a person, would grow so quickly from the sight of someone.

She smiled excitedly, causing his dick to twitch, and he gave a gentle nod, while with his other hand he waved. When she was past him, he caught at the corner of his vision, a security guard grabbing her. The line paused as people watched in fascination to see what had happened. He turned and saw her smile disappear as her happy eyes changed to fearfully wide, and her mouth opened and closed as she tried to ask the guard why she was being escorted out. She stumbled along as the large man pulled her away from the crowd of people.

성준 shook his head with a smirk and thought, 눌자.

KOREAN VOCABULARY:
성준 – Seong Jun – Seong Jun

지훈 – Ji-hun – Ji-hun
미쳤다 – michyeossda – crazy
준비됐음? – junbidwaess-eum? – are you ready?
집어쳐 – jib-eochyeo – cut the crap
눌자- nolja – let's play

CHAPTER THREE

Sophia's breathing rapidly quickened and she worried she would need a paper bag before she had a full-blown panic attack. She didn't want to argue with security, but she wanted to know why they were carting her away like she'd done something heinous.

The insanely broad man, who easily stood at six foot four, had his hand wrapped around her upper arm as he practically carried her down a creepy brightly lit white hallway.

Is this like concert jail?

"Why am I being brought here? What did I do?" Sophia struggled to get out from his grasp.

"You'll find out soon enough." He spoke monotonal, not even bothering to look down at her when he spoke.

Her gut sank. Maybe because she knew she was guilty of one thing.

Filming hi-touches was a no-no. They'd been instructed multiple times that recording was forbidden and to keep phones out of sight. But since Bridgette couldn't come, Sophia wanted to give her a little special something to try to make up for it. She shouldn't have done it, not only because she was told not to, but because CLAR1T hadn't consented to the video and she knew she wouldn't want someone filming her without her consent.

I fucked up.

"Listen, I'm sorry I filmed the hi-touch. I'll delete it, never post or share it anywhere. You can watch me do it. We can say it never happened and both go on our merry ways." She tried to reason with the man, who chuckled as he brought them to a halt in front of a light pinewood door.

Welp, I'm screwed. She had resigned herself to the fact she was going to be in deep shit for doing something so stupid. He grabbed the brushed silver handle, pushed it down, and pulled open the door. She was quickly tossed in, and before she could catch her balance, she heard the door slam and the click of a lock.

"Hey!" she shouted, grabbing the handle and jiggling it to confirm she was, in fact, locked in.

All this because I filmed a hi-touch?

Sophia banged on the door a few times before realizing it wasn't going to get her out of there. Taking her first gander around the room, there was a singular piece of furniture. A loveseat couch that looked hard and uninviting. Which was probably its point.

She had been on her feet for close to five hours, so even with the unpleasant look of the couch, she walked over to take a seat. Her suspicion of it being uncomfortable was confirmed as she bounced as if she'd sat in a bounce house, and the rough fabric scratched at her thighs.

The nervous tapping of her feet caused her thighs to continually rub the fabric, heightening her anxiousness. If they were trying to make her sweat, it was working.

What felt like an hour passed. Sophia turned her phone for what felt like the one hundredth time, to see the screen indicated it had been only a few minutes. She grumbled and tucked her phone into her bralette to stop her from checking the time constantly. It was at that moment she heard the door handle jiggle and finally open. She jumped to her feet when a man with a black wavy mop of medium-length hair that landed just above thick black brows, dark eyes, and the rest of his face behind a mask, walked in. He had on an oversized CLAR1T tour shirt and a pair of jogger sweatpants that all hid his physique. All she could gauge was he was broad and tall. At least six feet.

"If this is all over me taking a video of the hi-touch, I've learned my lesson. I will delete the video and never film another one again. I'll never take another picture or video at a concert. I swear." She pulled her phone out of its place in her bralette to show the man as she deleted it.

"I don't care about your video." His voice had a familiar Korean accent. She was sure she had heard it before, but there was no way it was who she thought.

"Then why am I being held here if it isn't because of the video?" She dropped her phone to her side as she waited to understand why she had been locked in that room if not for filming. His eyes grazed up and down her body, pausing at different points. She noticed them stop on her thighs, which made them clench together. Then her breasts, which made her cross her arms over them, and then her lips. His eyes stayed there for a long time, and she took her bottom lip between her teeth.

His gaze didn't scare her. That surprised her. It sent a nervous excitement coursing through her system. She could feel a warmth below her belly, and she was annoyed.

God, I've been reading too many dark romances lately. She scolded herself for finding a masked man, who kept her in a locked room and whose stare wandered hungrily and somewhat possessively over her body, sexy.

His eyes crinkled—she wondered if that meant he was smiling— as he brought his hands to the sides of his head, and the mask loosened on the front of his face. When the mask was removed, she stumbled back, her knees hitting the couch, and she fell onto the itchy fabric, bouncing several times in the process.

Holy shit. It's 성준. 성준 of CLAR1T.

CHAPTER FOUR

성준 loved hearing the small gasp that she made when she saw his face. Her parted lips had him imagining all the dirty things he wanted to do with that pretty little mouth.

Calm down, 성준, she hasn't even agreed to what you're about to propose.

"저는—"

"I know who you are," she cut him off with her breathy confession. Her voice was bewitching. It was like a siren calling him closer.

"Right." He reached to the back of his head, scratching the hair at the base of his head. He took a few steps closer to her seated frame and leaned forward, his hand grabbing the armrest of the couch, getting closer to her and taking in the sweet perfume that mixed with her sweat. She leaned back on the couch, her neck straining to look up at him, flaunting her gorgeous neck. Oh, how he wanted to have his hand around that neck, gently pressing as they both climaxed. 씨발. He had never been so turned on at the sight of someone.

"그럼..." 성준 decided to take the leap and reached out to touch her. His finger grazing her jaw, happy to see she didn't flinch.

God, her skin was even softer than he could've imagined. When he got to her chin, his thumb moved to her bottom lip, feeling her breath hitch as his finger smeared a bit of her gloss.

"You interested in fucking an idol?" he whispered pressing his thumb harder on her lip and pulling down. He prayed for her to say yes.

"Wha-wha-what?" she stuttered, shifting in her seat, but she didn't move away from his touch, which he took as a good sign.

He crouched down in front of her, her piercing green eyes following his every move.

"You gave the sign," his hand raising to mimic the downward V while his other hand went to her knee. *아주 부드러워*. He could see goosebumps rise on her skin when he touched her. Again, she didn't move away, which made him more hopeful she was going to say yes.

"T-th-the sign?" Her eyes went wide, her breathing quick. He smiled as he moved his hand between her knees and, with a gentle nudge from one of his fingers, her legs relaxed and opened a bit.

Good girl. He didn't need to speak and her body knew what to do. He needed her to answer him before he went any further though.

"Do you want to fuck an idol?" he asked more clearly.

"I—" She stopped, and he could almost see her thoughts running wild. The way her eyes darted around the room, and how her body shifted on the couch.

He was surprised. His cockiness had gotten the best of him, and he'd assumed any fan would be interested in having a night with an idol. Suddenly he was worried he wasn't going to get the answer he wanted. And he wasn't about to touch her if she didn't want it. He started to slide his hand from between her thighs when she squeezed them closed to keep it there.

"네." She whispered so softly, he wasn't sure he'd heard her.

"You're going to need to speak up. I won't do anything unless you are one hundred percent clear," he explained.

"네." This time, she spoke loud and clear.

That was all he needed to again use his fingers between her

thighs to push for her to open them. His hand moved farther up her thighs, and when he reached where he thought he would find panties he found two little buttons. He hooked his finger around and pulled for them to snap open giving him the access he wanted. His finger slipped into her wetness and she whimpered, her head falling back with a light thud as it hit the wall.

Fuck.

"Nothing under this sexy skirt and already wet for me?" He deeply growled, his cock straining at his pants, wanting to take the lead and bury himself inside her that instant. But he wanted to take his time with her. He was going to have the whole night.

"Do you want my fingers inside you?" His fingers swiped at her damp center, her hips jerking forward to get more from him.

"I want you to use words…" He paused realizing he hadn't taken a second to learn her name.

"Sophia," she moaned. "My name is Sophia."

"Sophia…" He pulled his fingers from her core. "예쁘다."

His fingers were coated in her arousal, and when the scent of her hit his nostrils, his patience was nearly torn to shreds.

"I need you to tell me you want me to continue. I need to know you want all of this because I plan to fuck you until you see stars."

He watched as her cheeks went from a soft pink to a bright red. But what was driving him mad with desire was the fact that her iridescent green eyes never left his. He loved that she was watching. He wanted her to watch. To unravel beneath him, on top of him, whatever position he put them in, he wanted her eyes watching as he made her cum repeatedly.

"Yes, please," she begged, moving her hips closer to the edge of the couch, spreading her legs wide.

That was all he needed to bring his fingers back between her legs.

KOREAN VOCABULARY:

저는 – jeoneun – I'm

씨발 – sshibal – fuck
그럼 – geurom – then
아주 부드러워 – aju budeuleowo – so soft
네 – nae – yes
예쁘다 – yeppeuda – pretty

CHAPTER FIVE

Sophia was trying to process how she ended up with the real life 성준, the same 성준 she had her fanatical fantasies of being between her legs, actually between her legs. His eyes had been devouring her body from the second he walked into the small room. It was an electric pull she couldn't deny, even without having fully seen his face.

No one had looked at her with that kind of fierceness, and it thrilled her. Before she could think more about being nervous for accepting his proposition of fucking her until she saw stars, he dropped to his knees and his fingers traced her inner thighs then outer, pushing her skirt up. She shivered as goosebumps raised all over her body.

Her hand instinctively grabbed his, scared he would want to stop if he saw her stomach rolls. She knew the Korean beauty standard was pale and thin, and her body wasn't it. His eyes left hers for the first time and went to her hands on his. He removed his hands from her hold before covering hers, grabbing them tightly and pressing them to the edge of the couch seat.

"Hold on to this, and don't let go," he commanded. "You won't disrupt me from my post-concert meal."

He licked his lips, released his hold on her hands, and continued pushing up her skirt.

"A-are you sure I'm the one you want to do this with?" Sophia slapped her hand over her mouth, scolding her self-consciousness, which was trying to cockblock her. His hands stopped and he removed them from her completely.

"If you're not comfortable, we can stop. You have every right to change your mind and I'm not about to force you to do something you don't feel at ease doing. We can leave and forget this moment happened." He leaned back onto his heels, holding his hands up in surrender.

"It's not…" She wanted to put into words the hundreds of thoughts fighting one another in her mind. 성준had just suggested he was about to eat her out. A fan, total stranger, after knowing her not even a few minutes.

"I'm me and you're you," is what her brain and mouth settled on.

"그래서?" He raised a perfectly shaped brow, indicating he was confused as to what she meant.

"Jesus Christ." She shook her head. "Look at you and then look at me."

He stared down at himself and when his eyes slowly roamed over her, the heated desire she felt when he first walked into the room emanated between them again.

"I *have* been looking at you." He grabbed her hand from where he placed it on the couch and tugged her torso closer. Their faces were centimeters from each other, and she took in his sharply pointed nose, his heart-shaped lips, and the small dimple on his cheek when he smirked. How many people had been that close to him? She wondered.

성준brought her hand down to his pants. A hard length touched her palm, and her eyes widened in shock. Not only due to the fact that he was hard, but his size. He closed his eyes as he pressed her hand harder onto his cock.

"I have been looking at you, Sophia." He moaned out, "And fuck, you're gorgeous."

She slowly closed her own eyes, and took the initiative to press and rub his dick. Her sharp inhale of once again stroking his impressive length was cut off by his lips on hers.

She almost jumped away out of shock, but he grabbed the side of her head, his fingers tangling in her hair, making sure she didn't shy away from something they clearly both wanted. His lips hungrily devoured hers, and finally her body chose to no longer hold back as she pressed her lips fiercely onto his. Her tongue met his and they danced with each other, evoking moans from both of them.

He pulled his lips away from hers, and she let out a whimper and wanted to slap her mouth for letting out such a pleading sound. Her eyes shot open, embarrassed and hoping he wasn't deterred by her moans. But she was surprised to see his eyes focused lower on her body. His hand went back to the space between her legs and pressed the inside of her thighs to spread them open again.

"Now, are you going to let me enjoy my meal?" 성준's voice was husky. "배고파."

Her jaw dropped, and her mind had gone out the window. Actually, there were no windows in the room, so it bounced around the room a few times before finally returning to tell her to give him an answer. She gave a quick nod.

"Good girl," he praised as he pushed her legs open wider. "Lift your ass for a second."

She shivered from his praise and followed his instructions, immediately leaning back so she could push her hips up, her ass leaving the couch. His hands went to her outer thighs to push her skirt up to her waist.

His lips grazed her inner thigh, the warmth causing her to close her eyes and let her head fall backward onto the back of the couch. Hot opened-mouthed kisses, his tongue swirling, his teeth nipping as he moved up to her center. As he neared, he sucked harder, and she knew it was to leave marks. *Holy shit, what a memory to remind me this actually happened.*

Before his lips met her center, his fingers gave her several swipes, and with every flick against her clit, her hips bucked, pressing his fingers closer to her opening.

"So eager." His breath was on her soaking core as she moaned a plea for him to do something. "And so responsive. Do you want my mouth on your cunt that badly?"

Fuck, his mouth was so filthy, and she felt herself get even more wet. She nodded quickly.

"I want you to say the word, Sophia." The warmth of his breath got even closer, his nose faintly pressed her clit.

"네. I want you to eat me out," she responded.

"씨발." He groaned before his mouth finally descended on her core, releasing a scream of pleasure. His tongue swiped at her clit one, two, three times, his lips surrounding it and sucking as he slipped a finger inside her. She ground up to ride his tongue and finger.

"So tight," he said before lapping at her clit again. He used his free hand to push her hips back down onto the couch, then grabbed her hand that had been gripping the edge, bringing it to his head. She opened her eyes and lifted her head to glance down to see his eyes meeting hers.

"Show me exactly what you want, 자기야." *자기야* . He'd called her a sweet name with that dirty mouth, and it made her own water. "Show me what makes you cum. I want to make you fall apart, your thighs crush my head. Suffocate me, 자기야." His dirty begging almost made her cum with no touch whatsoever. His finger curled inside her, and her hand gripped his hair, pressing his face into her.

She felt his smile. She could feel it on her cunt before his tongue joined his finger and he inserted a second finger, gently stretching her open to let his tongue plunge deeper.

"Oh fuck." She moaned at the new sensation of him stretching to eat her out.

No one had tried that before, and fuck, was it something she wanted going forward. His free hand moved up her belly, finding her breast and pinching her already pebbled nibble under the lingerie and bralette. She arched her back, giving in to the pain he was using to build her pleasure. She felt the vibration of his groan on her cunt.

"You taste so fucking good," he mumbled against her.

With every stroke of his tongue and pump of his fingers, she felt herself reaching the precipice of euphoria. Her legs started shaking, trying desperately to keep open. His mouth left her, his fingers pulled away, and as he pulled back, his face was red, his eyebrows scrunched, and his lips pursed angrily. His mouth and chin glistened with her arousal.

"I said I wanted you to crush me between your thighs as you cum, and yet you're trying so hard to keep them open." He leaned back onto his heels.

"미-미-미-미안해요." She tripped on her pronunciation.

"And now you're speaking formally when I have your taste on my lips?" He brushed his thumb across his bottom lip before sucking on it. "편하게 말해, 자기야."

He reached out to her torso and pinched her nipple. The pain caused her to bend forward, but it quickly subsided into pleasure.

"It seems like pain helps you get excited, Sophia." He twisted a little more, making her moan louder.

"날 믿어?" he asked.

"네?" She wasn't sure how she should answer. She knew him as a figment of her fanaticism, she never believed her delusion would become reality.

"Do you trust me?" he repeated in English.

"I-I—" *How can I?* He was, prior to ten minutes ago, an unobtainable idol. Someone she saw on a phone screen or on a stage. Not as someone who would be on his knees in front of her, someone who had paused eating her out in a greenroom at a concert venue to ask if she trusted him. It was a position she couldn't have imagined even in her wildest fantasies.

Can I trust him?

KOREAN VOCABULARY:

배고파 – baegopa – I'm hungry

자기야 – jagiya – term of endearment like "babe" or "honey"

미안해요 – mianhaeyo – I'm sorry

편하게 말해 – pyeonhage malhae – speak comfortably

날 믿어? – nal mid-eo? – do you trust me?

CHAPTER SIX

성준 could tell she was nervous to answer. She wasn't scared, but his question wasn't sitting well with her. While he had every intention of giving her pain for her pleasure, which he noticed got her more excited, her consent was key. He leaned forward onto his knees and grabbed her chin between his thumb and index finger.

Her lipstick was smeared all around her lips from their heated kiss, and he wondered what he looked like with her lipstick and arousal all over his own.

"It's okay," he calmly cooed. "Don't be scared. I'm not going to do anything you feel uncomfortable with. I just happened to notice you liked me pinching your nipples, and I wanted to help you cum."

"But…" she paused. "Why? Shouldn't this be about you?"

Those weren't the questions he was expecting.

"Why do you think this isn't?" He raised a brow.

"Because——"

"Because my cock isn't in you? Isn't in your cunt or mouth?" He had never been questioned so much by women he enjoyed. Hell, they loved the fact that the first thing he wanted to do was give *them* an orgasm before he was pounding into them, getting his own sweet release.

"Sophia, you're something special." He smirked, which set her face in confusion once more. A face he found extremely cute and had the burning desire to kiss again.

"You felt my dick, right?" he asked, and he watched her eyes dart down to his crotch, her cheeks burning that beautiful shade of red as she nodded. "So you felt how much I'm enjoying this?"

He leaned forward some more, their faces so close. The thumb that had been holding her chin brushed under her lip, smearing the lipstick even more. He leaned even farther, past her face and toward her ear.

"And given that you felt it, what makes you think this isn't about me?" he whispered against the shell of her ear, feeling her gently shiver. "Wanting to get you off..." He took her earlobe into his mouth, sucking gently as her hands went to his chest and grabbed at the fabric of his collar.

"Gets me off," he finished, and to make it clear how he felt, he cupped her cunt and pressed his palm to her clit, which elicited a moan and got her grinding up on his palm.

"Now, I'm going back down there to finish what I started." He swiped two fingers into her core, slipping them inside her as she gasped right by his ear. "You're going to cum and I am going to lick up every last drop, and then we can figure out what happens next."

He was nervous she wouldn't agree to it, an experience he'd never had before, but he saw her nod, and with a satisfied smirk, he moved back down her body.

His fingers still inside her, his tongue flicking her clit, he could feel her walls pulsing around his fingers, and he knew she was getting close. It hardened his cock in his pants, the fabric brushing his sensitive tip so it took everything in him not to cum in his pants.

"You want to cum?" he moaned out between flicks of her clit.

"네." She didn't hesitate.

Fuck. Something about her mixing Korean into her pleas had him wanting to make her cum even harder.

He pressed his thumb to her clit as he slid his tongue into her, and he felt her come undone around his fingers and tongue. Her legs clamped around his head, making him smile as he pulled his fingers out, replacing them with his mouth and pushing his tongue deeper to lap up her release while his thumb circled her clit to let her ride out her high. He sucked every last drop he could from her delicious cunt.

She was mouthwatering. The best he had ever tasted. In fact, he almost wanted to swear off eating out anyone else ever again because no one could compare.

As her legs lost their strength to hold him in place, he gave one final swipe of her sensitive clit, her hips bucking up as she spread her legs wide open.

He leaned back, using his thumb to wipe his mouth. He was about to lick his finger when he caught her eyes watching him. Her mouth hung open, her rapid breaths bouncing her gorgeous breasts.

"Do you want to taste yourself, Sophia?" he asked with a curious eyebrow raised. She bit her bottom lip.

Was it that she was afraid to tell him what she wanted? Was she worried he would think she was weird for wanting it?

He moved up to put his face in front of hers. "Sophia, you can tell me anything you desire. Anything you want to try. I am not going to judge you."

Her eyes focused solely on his lips, so he took the opportunity to bring his mouth to hers. Her tongue traced his bottom lip, which made them both moan loudly.

"I love the way you taste," he repeated between their kisses.

"Really?" she asked, surprised.

Why did she question every compliment he gave?

"I want to taste every part of your body, Sophia." He started to kiss down her neck "Every." Kiss "Single." Kiss. "Part."

He bit her neck, leaving a small mark; while they were only together for the night, he would leave something that she could remember for a short while afterward.

"Will you let me?" He pulled her in by her hips, her bare pussy rubbing against his sweatpants-covered dick.

Before she could answer, there was a knock on the door.

"성준 형, you in there?" he heard Minhwa loudly whisper.

"네," he responded calmly to soothe the panic he saw in Sophia's eyes. She tried to pull her skirt down and fix her appearance.

"The van is out back for us. They need us *all* on it in two minutes," Minhwa announced.

"아라. I'll be out in a minute." His focus didn't leave Sophia.

When he heard nothing else from outside, he knew Minhwa had started a timer and 성준 was running out of time.

"You need to get going." She tried to push him away.

"But I'm not done with you." He grabbed her chin so their eyes met. "You didn't answer my question."

"You have to leave in less than two minutes, 성준." As she spoke, a devious smirk hit her lips. "Can you be *that* quick?"

It was the first time she'd said his name, and holy fuck, it made his dick throb harder. He *needed* to hear her scream his name. He laughed at her challenge. With how hard he was, he might've been able to, but he wanted to spend several hours inside her.

"핸드폰 어디 있지?" He put out his hand.

"네?"

"핸드폰." He clapped his fingers against his palm impatiently, wanting her to put her phone in his hands.

She searched around and found the phone on the couch cushion beside her and gave it to him. He opened it to her messaging app, added his number, and texted his hotel info, most importantly his room number. He felt the vibration in his pocket, confirming he now had her number and could play it off as someone on the team he asked information from.

"You're right. I can't be that quick." He smirked as he handed the phone back to her. "And I don't want to be."

"이게 뭐야?" Her eyes darted between the text back and him several times.

"If you want to continue what we started here, meet me there in an hour. If not, I'll understand." He sighed, hoping she wouldn't choose the latter. "Disappointed, but understood."

He went to stand and remove himself from her luscious body

when he saw the glistening of her pussy and the mess she had made on the couch.

He searched for something to help clean her up, and he felt around clothes to find the mask he had in his pants pocket.

"미안, this is all I have." He reached down and swiped what his mouth had missed on her, and she jumped back. "미안," he repeated.

"It's not you, it's the texture of the mask." She laughed sweetly. Sweeter than those fake laughs he heard from most people around him, trying hard to be something to him and his group members. Hers was carefree, the least nervous laugh he'd heard from her since they'd met.

성준 shoved the mask back into his pocket to throw it out when he could, and as he geared up to ask her about his request, there was another, slightly louder knock at the door.

"형," Minhwa begged.

"I'm coming!" he shouted back. He put out his hand for Sophia to take. She slipped hers into his gently. They were so soft but strong. He helped her stand.

"I hope to see you later, Sophia." 성준 leaned in to kiss her cheek, too nervous now to await a response. He turned and walked out of the room to see Minhwa standing with big wide doe eyes, knowing he'd interrupted something and trying to get a look into the room.

"가자." 성준 nudged him toward the hallway leading to the exit. They walked in silence, 성준's mind on the woman he'd just walked away from, and he honestly didn't care why Minhwa was silent.

When they got to the large metal doors, he could hear the screams that came through them. 성준 took a deep breath and reached for the door, but Minhwa put out his arm, hitting 성준 across his chest.

"We need to put our masks on." Minhwa grabbed his from his pocket and covered his nose and mouth.

성준 grumbled but knew it was for safety purposes, and he

pulled it out of his pocket. But once he felt the damp nature, he remembered where his mask had just been.

Jesus fucking Christ.

"Do you have an extra mask?" he asked Minhwa.

"아니. Yours looks fine. Come on we gotta go." He went to push open the door, forcing 성준to apply the mask to his face.

Sweet torture assaulted his senses when he breathed in Sophia's sweet scent. Her desire coating his mask was his new favorite perfume.

He wanted so much more time with her. He hoped she would meet him at his room so he could see her body on top of his, underneath his—fuck, even against the wall of his hotel room, even if his groupmates could hear them next door. His cock deep inside her as he grabbed her deliciously plump hips and they reached their highs countless times.

Deep breaths to try to keep himself calm just added to his torture. All he wanted was his face to be buried in her pussy again. Followed by his cock. His cock, which was painfully tucked into his sweatpant waistband, was so sensitive with every step, he felt he might cum on his stomach under his shirt.

If she didn't show, at least he had his mask covered in her to help him jack off to.

He couldn't focus on waving to the fans who stood outside, waiting for them behind barriers and happily jumping at the sight of him and Minhwa. His mind was focused on the vixen that was Sophia. He was thanking the world's weird kismet energy that she had been the only person ever to follow his tweet request.

"형, 괜찮아?" Minhwa asked as they climbed onto the bus.

성준 gave a quick nod and closed his eyes to wait for the van to get to the hotel, where hopefully he would receive a knock on his door from Sophia.

한 시간. I have to wait just one hour.

KOREAN VOCABULARY:
성준 형 – Seong Jun hyung – Seong Jun hyung (Hyung is a term

used between males when the one being spoken to is older. It represents closeness between to two.)

아라 – ahlah – I know

핸드폰 어디있지? – haendeupon eodiissji – where is your cellphone?

이게 뭐야? – ige mwoya? – what is this?

가자 – gaja – let's go

아니 – ani – no

괜찮아? – gwaenchanh-a? – are you okay?

한 시간 – han shigan – one hour

CHAPTER SEVEN

S ophia walked down the block, convincing herself she was in an extremely vivid dream. No way did 성준 of CLAR1T eat her out in a greenroom backstage after his concert and then invite her back to his hotel room for more. *What a dream! What a real-feeling dream.*

Her body reminded her that it wasn't just a dream. With every step, her legs felt like jelly. Reminding her that he'd made her cum so hard, she was surprised she had been able to stand afterward. It took a bit of time, if she was being honest. After he left the room, she fell back on the couch, her legs shaking and heart racing as she thought about how he'd commanded her body, how sexy he'd looked every time he glanced up at her from between her legs, his fingers curling inside her as his tongue flicked at her clit and lapped her up.

She was wet all over again. Could she allow herself to enjoy what he was offering? He'd made it clear he liked her body. Which was a nice surprise, considering the Korean beauty standard and how she didn't match it.

As her mind wandered and questioned, she stopped walking. Her brain caught up to her body, causing her to look around and find out where she was. She examined her surroundings and caught the lit-up name from the building to her right-hand side. A hotel.

성준's hotel. While her mind was contemplating the pros and cons, her body had made its decision.

It wanted 성준.

She took a deep breath and entered the building. It was a plain entryway, with the reception desk on one side and a small seating area for guests or friends of guests to sit and wait. Farther past the plain entryway was a small elevator bank. She pressed the button and, with a ding, the doors parted for her to enter. She climbed in, and as the elevator climbed the several floors to his room, she calmed her heartbeat as best she could.

The elevator slowed, finally coming to a complete stop and announcing the floor as the doors opened. Sophia walked to the room number he had put in the text. She was about to knock, but she stopped, realizing the noise could possibly notify the other rooms around, which she assumed were the other members, crew, and most likely managers. While she had never been in this situation, she knew idols had their rules.

She opened his text and messaged him to let him know she was outside his door. She could hear the ding of him receiving the message in his room, making her heart flutter. And then the door opened, revealing a bright smile and excited eyes. She was comforted by the fact that he looked so excited for her to be standing at that door.

His hand reached out to her, and the second she placed hers in it, she was pulled into the room and pressed against the hotel room wall, the door closing behind them and shutting out the rest of the world. His mouth crushing hers, his hands roaming over her body. They grabbed at her thighs, squeezing them and drawing a moan into his abrasive kiss.

"Sitting in that van was torture," he said as he pressed his body against her, leaning down to grab her thighs to lift her and wrap her legs around his waist. She could feel how thin he was compared to her, and panic set in that he wasn't used to lifting someone as big as her. She pushed to try and get him to put her down.

She tried to move her legs, but with every wiggle, he gripped them harder.

"성준." She pulled her lips back from his, her head hitting the wall. "You should put me down. I don't want to hurt—"

"Does it feel or look like I have a problem holding you?" He cut her off as he pressed his body into her, and she could feel his hard cock beneath his sweatpants, brushing at her entrance.

"Your scent drove me crazy in that van." His hand reached into his pocket and pulled out the mask he had used to wipe her clean. "I had to wear this and pretend like my cock wasn't about to ruin my pants before we got back here, where I prayed you would meet me."

His lips began to trace down her chin, jaw, and neck. They nipped and teased, and she gave up any fight about him holding her up.

"Why did you wear that mask?" she asked as she felt heat building throughout her body.

"I didn't have a choice." He brought it to his face and took a deep inhale. "And I loved every fucking second of that torture."

Holy shit. He is raunchy.

He smiled so wide, it made her laugh.

"You're nothing like what I expected," she admitted.

"What did you expect?" He raised a brow as he leaned his body closer to her again. His nose grazed her, and in a very different move, a much gentler move, he pressed his lips to the tip of her nose.

"Well I only know what you show. From your concerts, vlogs, social media posts. The stuff curated to *make* me and other CLAR-voyants have an image of you and to fall in love with that image." She blushed admitting to "loving" him.

"You're right. If fans found out how much I enjoyed eating you out and how I plan to do it several more times tonight, they prob-ably wouldn't be too thrilled." His laughter was boisterous and vibrated against her chest.

"I guess yes, that is part of it." She chuckled along with his laughter. "But I guess what I'm trying to say is, you're…normal."

"Normal?" He raised a brow and his laughing slowly stopped.

"So what we're doing here is a normal occurrence for you?" He cupped her cheek, his thumb playing across her bottom lip. "I'm not surprised by that. I'm sure men are banging down your door for a chance with you. You're fucking gorgeous."

She got shivers every time he cursed. It added to the things she knew about him that most CLARvoyants didn't. Maybe a different one at every stop? That seemed like typical behavior for attractive musicians. Hell, even the unattractive.

"Where is your mind, 자기야?" he asked as he pinched her bottom lip between his two fingers.

"미안, in the same thought process of me thinking you're normal, I also thought about the fact that you're an idol and have people throwing themselves at you." She laughed nervously and covered her face as it turned a bright shade of red.

"야,야,야…" He grabbed one of her wrists, tugging it away from her face. "I'm not going to lie. I have been with a number of different people since debuting, and since we only have one or two nights in each stop on this tour…" He trailed off.

She knew what he was saying. She was only there with him for the night. He was making it known what their "status" was.

"If that isn't what you expected or what you feel comfortable with, let me know. I won't go any further." He let go of her legs, letting them drop down to the floor as he stepped back to create space between the two of them.

She wasn't upset or surprised by what he said. She was happy he was being up-front about it.

"This might sound like a line to try to convince you to stay and let me worship your body, but I've never been so turned on by some-one. To be so attracted to not only your body, but what is going through your mind. I'm desperate to hear your every thought." He reached out to take her hand and bring it to his lips.

"성준…" She trailed off, and he groaned against her wrist as he pressed her against the wall once again.

"Just you saying my name drives me insane." He spoke as he kissed up her arm.

성준 wanted to worship Sophia. He'd practically said it himself.

She was trying to wrap her mind around that. Maybe by the end of the night she would.

And with that thought, she knew she had made up her mind. But she also knew since it would only be one night, they needed to discuss the things that were on and off the table.

"If we're going to do this, we need to talk." She grabbed his hand and shimmied free from him pressing against her, then led them to sit on the bed.

"Talk?" he asked.

"네, about things we like, don't like. Our kinks, stuff like that," she explained.

His eyes lit up when she said the word "kinks."

"Do you want to go first?" he asked.

"I enjoy praise, but degradation is also a turn-on. I think it depends on the situation. Being tied up, I've only tried once or twice, and it was interesting. I just don't think my partner was a fan, so I don't think I got the full experience. I would be open to trying it again." Sophia laughed nervously when she caught him watching her closely as she spoke. "That's some of my basics. Now you tell me some of yours."

He let go of her hand and rubbed his palms along his sweat-pants. His one leg began to bounce as he let out a loud exhale.

"This is a first for me." 성준 chuckled, bringing one of his hands to his neck and rubbing nervously. "I enjoy similar types of things to what you said. Since we're being open and honest, while I like those things, I've never tried them. My partners never expressed the same interests."

"I'm open to trying a lot of things." She reached for his hand to comfort him. She was surprised by his nervousness, considering how he'd handled himself in the greenroom. "If there are things you haven't been able to do with other partners, we can try them together."

"Sophia." His voice was shaky with lustful hunger. "Waiting for you this last hour, I have been picturing all the things I want to do to you. All the positions I want to have you in."

"Prove it then." Sophia knew what she wanted, and she only

had this one chance to have him. She brought the hand she had been holding to her chest. Her free hand reached over to his cock.

A fire lit in his eyes, and he pressed his cock up into her hand as his forehead met hers, "Oh 자기야."

"네?" she whispered just before he crushed his mouth onto hers. He leaned over to her, forcing them both to fall onto the bed.

Their hands were everywhere, all over each other. His hands went under her skirt to snap the buttons of the bodysuit so he could pull the body suit over her head. He paused to take in her breasts in only the bralette. A sexy grin played across his lips. He dipped his head between her breasts as she reached behind her and unclasped the bralette to free her breasts for him to enjoy more thoroughly.

She was desperate to feel his skin on hers. She reached under his shirt to push it up and pull it off, messing up his hair and making it look deliciously fluffy and she was excited to run her hands through it throughout the night. She instinctively lifted her hips and he happily pulled her skirt down as she simultaneously pulled down his sweatpants. Bare to each other she looked down the length of his body making a mental note of his lean torso, down to his large cock.

His naked body pressed against hers, his cock pushing into her stomach. She was finally able to take in the full length of it. Long and hard, and she was desperate for it to be inside her, giving her the best orgasms she ever had in her life. She grabbed it, her hand moving up and down, enjoying how big he was.

성준's hands grabbed her breasts, squeezing them hard before taking her nipples between his index fingers and thumbs and twisting. She yelped in shock but leaned into the pain, knowing how much she would enjoy it from when he had done the same in the greenroom. It was something she had done to herself when with partners who were lackluster, or when she had to get herself off with her vibrator.

"You want more of that?" His lips trailed down her neck. "You like the way that makes you feel?" He bit her neck, no longer holding back like she believed he had in the greenroom.

"네." She tugged his cock as she tried to shimmy up to get his length to her entrance.

"Oh 자기야, you're gonna have to wait just a bit longer for that." He smirked as he moved away from her and climbed off the bed. Confused, she sat up, her eyes following him as he walked to the end of the bed and then stood in front of her, his cock right at mouth height. She salivated at the thought, but he dipped down his hands on her one thigh, and before she could ask what he was doing, he spun her around like she was a rag doll, and she was face down on the bed.

"On all fours," he commanded. She turned her body a bit to catch a glimpse of his face. His eyes raking over her naked frame set alight the thrill inside hers, but also a hint of self-consciousness. She instinctively went to cover her tummy, but he grabbed her wrist.

"Don't you dare hide yourself. I want to see every piece of you. I want to find every place that makes you moan so I can leave my mark, make you *mine*." His voice had dropped an octave.

The word "mine" hung in the air between them for a few seconds. He stepped closer to the bed. "I'm not going to repeat myself, Sophia."

Her name on his lips could command her to commit arson if he so desired it. But at that moment he wanted her on all fours. So she rolled back fully onto her stomach and lifted herself to plant her knees near the edge and her hands on the bed.

"That's my girl," he praised, and she shivered under the admiration. She felt his hand grip her hip and pulled her back toward him, and then she felt his dick press between her ass cheeks. She leaned farther back to grind herself against him and get some relief. That relief was cut short when a loud clap echoed in the room, and a stinging pain burned on her left butt cheek. She jumped away from him.

"미안, Sophia. 미안. I thought— You— I should've—" he stumbled as he reached out to touch her but stopped himself. "Fuck, please…"

His hand went into his thick hair, tugging it in distress. She wasn't frightened, just surprised.

Instead of saying anything, she moved back toward him, into position.

"Sophia——"

"I'm not afraid of you, 성준," she explained. "I was caught by surprise."

"If you don't trust me——"

"Please, 성준," she interrupted. "I want more."

"If it's too much, tell me to stop. Immediately. I will stop." His hand stroked the tingling spot on her ass.

"I will." She nodded. "Please, 성준, I——"

She was cut off by a loud slap that came down on her other ass cheek. She dropped down to muffle her screams into the bedding.

"Absolutely not, 자기야." He spoke through what sounded like gritted teeth. As she felt his fingers run from the base of her skull to the back of her head, gripping her hair and pulling to lift her head off the sheets. "I want to hear those moans loud and clear."

Sophia was getting more wet by the second. She craved his rough, dominating hands. His commands alone could send her over the edge. Another loud slap on her ass, her cry of pleasure, and his hand soothing her cheeks before slipping between her legs to rub her clit. She backed up to him, wanting more of his expert strokes.

"Fuck, Sophia," 성준 groaned, his fingers slipping inside her. "You're so fucking wet. You're dripping. I want to taste it again."

His fingers left her core and she felt empty. She moaned her displeasure, backing herself into him to try to make him punish her again, but instead, she heard a sucking noise. She turned her head to see behind her, and there he was, fingers in his mouth.

His eyes caught hers watching him, and he smirked.

"자기야, you're so much more adventurous than I anticipated." He slipped his fingers back inside her. "Be a good girl and use my fingers."

She moved to guide his fingers to the right spot that sent waves of pleasure through her. Gripping the bedspread, she moaned. His hand left her hair and slapped her ass.

"You use my fingers so well. Can't wait to get my cock in that sweet cunt of yours." *Slap!* "You can't cum until I tell you."

Another slap that had her pushing herself harder onto his

fingers. She felt them curl inside her, and her arms shook so much, she dropped to her elbows. "성준," she cried out.

"응, 자기야, tell me what you want. Let me see if I'll be willing to give it to you." His lips were just above her ass, kissing up her spine and then back down and onto her ass, where she knew she would have bright red handprints and be sore tomorrow morning.

"More," she pleaded.

"More?" he asked. "More what?"

"Everything." She was too high on pleasure, she couldn't think clearly as to what she wanted. She just knew she needed more.

"Hmmmm…" He curled his fingers inside her again, and she pushed back onto them. "More…fingers?"

A third finger joined the two already inside her, filling her even more. But it wasn't enough.

"I can feel you squeezing around them. Keep riding them, 자기 야." He continued pushing the fingers into her and curling them when she pressed onto them.

"More…spanking?" He slapped one of her cheeks, then the other.

She cried out his name, getting closer to her second orgasm of the night.

"More holes?" His thumb pressed against her back hole, and she pushed into it, letting the tip get sucked in a bit.

"I'm-I'm—" She couldn't get the words out as her mind started to go blank from the euphoria building.

"You're not going to cum," he hissed. "Not until I'm ready." Once again, his fingers left her, and she was ready to argue when the bed bounced. She turned her head, unable to see, and then she felt a tap on her clit that almost buckled her knees. She dropped her head to see his body between her legs his face right at her center.

"You should already know how much I love your sexy thighs crushing me while you cum." His finger ran through her slit, and it took all her strength not to collapse on top of him.

"Sophia." He moved his head so his eyes met hers. "You can cum. But only if you do it when you sit on my face."

"Are you—"

She was cut off by his hands grabbing her ass and pulling her down onto his face. His nose brushed her sensitive clit as his mouth once again devoured her cunt. His tongue pushed into her fast as his nose continued to rub her clit. She tried to lift off him, worried he wasn't able to breathe, but every time she did, she was met with his fingers pinching her or his hand slapping her ass.

"성-성-성준." She stuttered as his assaulting pace caused her knees to shake.

"That's it, Sophia," he mumbled against her cunt. "Cum for me, 자기야."

He moved his mouth to her clit and sucked hard before taking his teeth and gently nipping, and for the next several seconds her mind was black. She could somewhat remember screaming his name and pressing her hips down onto his face. She shivered, her knuckles white from gripping the sheets as sheer pleasure rocked her body.

When the high dwindled and her senses began to return, she lifted her hips to see 성준 laying there, not moving. She panicked, thinking she did, in fact, suffocate him and had killed a member of her favorite K-pop group. She wondered how they would tell the world he died. Killing an idol was not on her bingo card for the year.

When she was able to get a good look at his face, it wasn't what she expected. He had a dopey grin on his face, his eyes half-lidded, his cheeks bright red. He looked drunk.

"괜찮아?" she asked.

When he turned his head up, his eyes meeting hers, his expression remained adorably dopey. He pushed himself farther up the bed, under her body, until their faces were at the same level.

"Come here." He waved before cupping her face to bring her lips to his. Once again tasting herself on his lips. His tongue swiped at her bottom lip, and she gave him the access he wanted as he rolled them over to put himself above her.

His hand grabbed one breast, and his lips traced down to meet his hand and take her nipple into his mouth.

"I love your breasts pouring out of my hand." He bit the pink peak, making it harden.

"I love those thighs crushing me, your hips dropping to press me harder into you. Fuck…it's going to be hard to let you leave tomorrow morning."

His admission sent her heart racing faster than when he had made her cum so hard she blacked out.

"성준." She cupped his cheek, taking in how handsome he was so close up. Not just performing on stage, but outside of all the glamour.

"If all I can have is tonight, I'm going to take my time." He leaned in to kiss her softly.

It was the second most tender thing he'd done, and she responded with similar tenderness. She wasn't sure he had meant to say all of that out loud, but if he meant what he said, she was going to let him take everything he wanted from her.

KOREAN VOCABULARY:

야,야,야 – ya, ya, ya – hey, hey, hey

CHAPTER EIGHT

Something about Sophia made 성준 pause. He had his own ideas of what he wanted from just one night. His partially admitting he wanted her for more than that night was unintentional, but it also wasn't untrue. Saying it would be hard to let her leave tomorrow never fell so easily from his lips before.

And the crazy part was, she seemed ready and willing to hear his thoughts as well as act out any of his desires and kinks. He enjoyed how open she was about what she liked and what she wanted to explore. She let him try things that none had before and even begged for more. She liked the wilder side, something he had images of when he was alone, with just his hand. His plan was to let them both quench their thirst for their needs as much as possible, given their time constraint.

"Will you let me try something more interesting?" he asked.

"*More* interesting?" She raised a brow, but with a sexy smirk that told him she was very much keen and very much willing.

He sat up, got off the bed, and walked over to his suitcase to grab a few ties from his wardrobe. When he turned back to explain, he was shocked to see her on her knees on the floor beside the bed.

"무슨—"

"You made me cum with your mouth, twice." Sophia's smile was wicked and made his mind delirious with desire. His dick pulsed, somehow getting ever harder. "I want to do the same."

She licked her lips as her eyes went down 성준's body, stopping at his cock, and a hunger took over his body.

He took the few steps to meet her within the tiny hotel room and grabbed her chin to raise her face to stare up at him. Oh, he was most certainly going to fuck that pretty little mouth of hers.

"Put your hands behind your back," he ordered, and she wasted no time in following his instruction. He walked up behind her and crouched down, his fingers running over the length of her arms, loving the way she shivers and goosebumps appear on her skin.

His hand grabbed her arms and, using one of his ties, he wrapped them around her wrists and pulled to make a knot. She let out a squeak, and he could see her hips drop trying to find some kind of friction.

His fingers, once finished tying her wrists, slipped between her butt cheeks. Her slickness coated her puckered hole, and she leaned back into his fingers, letting one slip in up to the first knuckle, which only made him want to push it even farther in.

"I can't wait to put my cock in every hole you let me and have you ride it just as enthusiastically as you do my fingers and face." He spoke on the shell of her ear, catching the sound of her shuddered breath.

He removed his finger and stood to walk back around and stand in front of her. Her big tits were begging to have his cum on them, and he was ready to make a mess. He reached down to grab her tits pushing them together.

"Can I—"

"You don't need to ask, 성준. I will tell you if I can't handle something." Her sultry voice made him feel comfortable with what he thought most people would consider "unusual" desires.

"It's not something I've done before," he explained, "but it's something I want to try with you."

She leaned closer to him, her tongue slipping out and sliding up the slit at the head of his cock. They moaned simultaneously.

"Do it, 성준. I can handle it." That devious freaking smile was going to be the end of him.

It was a command he was happy to follow, but he was supposed to be the one making the rules. He wrapped his hand in her hair and pulled her head back.

"My cock is going to be in your mouth soon enough. Don't get ahead of yourself." He watched her breath catch as she bit her bottom lip to control herself.

His mouth watered, filling with a nice amount of saliva. *A perfect lubricant.* Once he had enough, he spit onto her chest, watching it slip between her breasts. He released her hair and used his hands to press her tits together, then let his cock slide between them.

"씨발," he groaned out as he pumped his cock between her breasts. He could've cum after the first pass like a damn teenager. And he wasn't even inside her yet. When he looked down at her, he caught her eyes solely focused on his cock, her mouth hanging open with a hunger to have it in there.

Not yet, 자기야.

"나좀봐." He breathed out as he pumped into her breasts again. Her emerald eyes glimmering with excitement and hungered lust turned up to meet his. They watched each other, and in his peripheral, he could see her try to move her arms. His dick got harder at how hot it was to be in control.

He lacked control in most other aspects of his life. Everything was regulated. What he ate, where he went, even who he hung out with. When he'd joined the company, he was young and naive, thinking he would be a celebrity who enjoyed all the finer things in life with more freedom than he had at home. But when he actually started the training process, he realized it was nothing like his imagination. Long hours of school, dance practice, vocal coaching, manners and etiquette classes daily. Barely any time to relax. And when he finally debuted, there was the added TV performances, fan sign events. Him getting more than two hours of sleep a night was not common.

He had thought about leaving. But he couldn't without incurring an insane breach of contract cost that he couldn't afford.

So he gave up his control.

But having Sophia on her knees, willing to do anything he wanted, listening to his commands with aroused attentiveness, gradually giving him a small semblance of his power back. With every pump between her tits, his pleasure built. But he wouldn't cum. His enjoyment came from the pain of edging himself.

"Open your mouth, Sophia."

Not only did she open her mouth, but she stuck her tongue out eagerly, ready to receive him.

"You're such a good fucking slut." The words slipped out of his mouth before he could catch them. He leaned back to gauge her reaction, worried he had crossed a line. She did say she enjoyed degradation, but…

His panic was cut by her shuffling closer to him and taking the head of his cock in her mouth.

"Sophia, I—" He couldn't finish the sentence as she slid her mouth down his whole cock. He could feel the back of her throat, her tongue swirling as she pulled back and their eyes met again. He could see the hint of a smile on her lips that were still wrapped around his cock. She was hungry to please him.

성준 pushed his cock back into her mouth, feeling and hearing her gag, spit falling from the corners of her mouth. "Take it all, 자기야."

She obediently listened, and while gagging every time he pushed himself into her mouth, her tongue swiped and swirled as best it could.

Who is this woman?

"You like choking on my cock this much?" he asked roughly as he pumped into her.

She moaned, sending vibrations through his cock, and he knew he wasn't going to last much longer if he stayed in her mouth.

A loud vibration came from the desk beside them. He saw his phone light up and her head started to turn, but he grabbed her hair to keep her focused on the task at hand.

"Keep sucking." He smirked as he leaned over to grab the phone, swiping to answer the call.

"응?" he answered.

"형." Minhwa's voice came from the other end. Second time that night he'd interrupted 성준's fun. "뭐해?"

"Busy, Minhw-hwa," he stumbled as she pushed his cock farther into her mouth.

"Want to meet up in Eunho's room?" Minhwa asked.

"밥 먹고 있어." The phrase he knew would get Minhwa and the rest of the members to leave him alone for the rest of the night.

"아." Minhwa's voice had filled with mischief. "뭐 먹어?"

"소떡소떡," he responded as Sophia's mouth began to meet his thrusts.

"맛있게 먹어." Minhwa hung up quickly after that.

The boys had a code. Rules were rules, but 성준 had quickly learned he wasn't the only one in the group who had wanted to get some of their control back. They came up with a system. If they wanted some free time to do whatever it was they wanted to do, they would say they were eating. When asked what they were eating, they all had their own food phrase that told the rest of the group to cover for the one disappearing.

To their management, it looked like the boys were going out to grab something to eat, but to the boys, it was their small time for freedom and a tiny sense of normalcy.

She moaned again, the vibrations making it unbearable to keep himself at bay. The lower part of his spine was screaming at him to pull out or he would cum too soon.

"I'm gonna—" He was trying to pull his cock out of her mouth, but she followed him, pushing him back in and sucking hard. He grabbed her hair to pull her away, but instead she pushed herself forward, his cock hitting the back of her throat again, and his release couldn't be controlled.

She gagged, coughing a bit with his cock still in her mouth as she swallowed everything he loaded into her.

"Fucking hell," he groaned out as she finally let his cock fall from her mouth. A satisfied smile crept onto her lips. He wanted to praise her for taking it all, but with how she chose to fight his control of the situation, he had a sneaking suspicion she would rather be punished instead.

He grabbed her jaw, her lips forcefully being puckered by his grip, and pulled up so she was forced to stand in front of him.

"I bet you're proud of yourself." He raised a brow, and her smushed smiled indicated that she was. "But I wanted to cum on your pretty tits, and you chose not to follow my orders." He pulled her face closer, their lips only a breath apart.

"Good whores get rewards. Bad ones…" He turned them to push her back onto the bed. She couldn't brace herself with her hands still tied behind her back. "Get punished."

Korean Vocabulary:

무슨— - museum-- – what--

나좀봐 – najombwa – look at me

응 – eung – used as acknowledgement, like yes

뭐해? – mwohae? – what are you up to?

밥 먹고 있어 – bab meoggo iss-eo – I'm eating

뭐 먹어? – mwo meog-eo? – what are you eating?

소떡소떡 – sotteoksotteok – an abbreviated name for a street food that consists of mini sausages and tteok (rice cake) with a sweet and spicy sauce on a skewer

맛있게 먹어 – mas-issge meog-eo – enjoy your meal

CHAPTER NINE

Is it wrong to be excited about being punished? Sophia thought.

It was worth it. 성준's cock in her mouth was stimulating, and hearing the moans she elicited from him made her want to continue sucking and choking on it for as long as she could. When she felt his cum start to fill her throat, she was happy she disobeyed his hair pulling. He made her cum in his mouth, she wanted the same reward of his cum in hers.

And when she was tossed onto the bed, she was willing to take what he wanted to dole out.

"You look excited to be punished." His smirk was pure sex as he placed his knees on the bed. He pulled out another tie and placed it over her eyes, lifting her head to tie it around the back. She felt his lips on her ear, which made her breath catch, and with that breath came his scent. Sweat and flowers. It fit him. She wanted the scent to be ingrained in her memory for years to come.

"I'm not going to let you see how much pleasure I get from your screams," he whispered, his hands letting go from knotting the tie at the back of her head, before they very gently traced down her neck to her chest, where his fingers whispered a touch, brushing her nipples. Without her sight, his touch was more addictive.

The feather-like contact with her nipples made her arch her chest upward for more and that's when his fingers pinched and twisted, causing her to cry out, wanting to leap from the bed, but her arms were behind her back and she couldn't see anything.

"You're being needy, wanting to get *your* pleasure." He released her nipples and his hands cupped her large breasts, squeezing hard. "This is your punishment. I get the pleasure and you..." He trailed off as he let go of her breasts.

His lips went to one of her pebbled nipples and sucked hard, causing her to cry out again, and she restrained herself from arching into his mouth. The pain was just as deliciously, sinfully pleasurable as him eating her out in the greenroom of the concert venue.

"You are going to get so close to an orgasm but never get to feel it. That's your punishment for being a disobedient slut."

She had always wanted to try degradation and roughness, but none of the guys she had been with seemed the type. When she even mentioned simple things like dirty talk, they were too nervous to try, or if they did, they struggled and ended up giving up and just doing what they wanted. When she had finally gotten one guy to try tying her up, he ended up taking off the restraints, saying he didn't like seeing her squirm, even though it was what she wanted.

"That's a bit better," he whispered, his lips tripping over her nipple, and if it could've gotten harder, it would.

"Jesus," she moaned out.

"아니야. 난은 성준아. That's the name you need to scream and moan," he growled, biting down on her other nipple. "I want to worship this body as much as I want to punish it." His lips ghosted down her torso.

She could feel his breath skim her stomach. He was right about the torture part. Her body wanted more than the feather-light touches. She preferred the pain, if she was being honest with herself. She could feel how wet she got when he twisted her nipples. And he clearly knew that.

His lips kissed her stomach just above her center and she instinctively tried to shy away. Him being so close to her rolls scared her. In the greenroom, she'd had her skirt to hide the insecurity. And on her knees he wasn't able to see much past her breasts, which again hid her stomach. But he continued to touch and kiss her stomach. She tried to move again, but he pushed her hips back onto the bed with a loud growl.

"You're being a bad girl, Sophia." He grabbed her thighs, spreading them, and she felt his mouth on her wet center.

"미-미-미안, I-I-just—" She was trying to put her self-consciousness of being totally naked in front of someone into words, but his lips sucking on her clit was making words extremely hard to form.

But his mouth left her, as did his hands and his weight off the bed. The soft light of the room blinded her as her blindfold was removed, and her eyes had to adjust to see that 성준 stood off to the side of the bed.

"I don't want you to be afraid of me." He spoke with a tone of concern. "Are you afraid of me?"

"I-I'm not." She was desperate to convince him.

"You just flinched at my touch. You said you would tell me when you couldn't handle it." He pointed to her thighs, which were still wide open. She closed them and moved to try and cover herself up, but her arms were still tied behind her back. "I won't touch you if you're scared."

He leaned closer to her and his hand slipped under her to untie her wrists.

"성준아." Her hands fell from the restraints as he walked to his suitcase to toss the ties back in. "제발 그만해." She begged.

"Sophia…" His voice was strained, and he wouldn't turn to face her, which made her heart clench. "Once you're dressed and ready, I'll pay for a taxi to take you wherever you want to go."

She climbed off the bed and walked over to stand in front of him. She cupped his cheek to get his attention on her. His eyes were sad. The light of excitement she had seen before was gone.

"I'm sorry. It had nothing to do with you. I'm self-conscious about my stomach and—"

"왜?" he cut her off.

"뭐?" she asked confused.

"Why are you self-conscious about your stomach?" He brought a hand to her tummy, his fingers running across it.

The question surprised her because to her the answer was simple. The world. While she owned her curves in clothes, when naked, it was a different story. And when she would go on dates, she would see the men's disappointment. She never lied about her weight, never hid it, but when they saw her in person, the curves they claimed to love weren't *her* curves.

"Sophia...자기야." He brought his hands to her cheeks, and then she felt him swipe under her eye, and a cool wetness spread across her cheek.

She hadn't realized she had started to cry.

"I enjoy every part of your body, but if you can't love yourself, my words are pointless." He leaned down and kissed her forehead. "You need to see how gorgeous you are."

He kissed her eyelids.

"Can I try to help?"

KOREAN VOCABULARY:

아니야. 난은 성준아. – aniya. nan-eun seongjun-a. – No. I'm Seong Jun

제발 그만해 – jebal geumanhae – please stop

왜? – wae? – why

뭐? – mwo? – what?

CHAPTER TEN

성준 could see tears forming in Sophia's eyes, and she was trying to hide her trembling bottom lip, but he noticed the movement instantly. She hadn't said a word, but he could tell there was something from her past that affected her thought process in the present. She was unsure of herself when he had first met her in the greenroom. She had implied that the way she looked and the way he did were not a match. Meanwhile from the second he had seen her make the sign he had posted on social media, his eyes couldn't leave her because of the naughty images of them coming together perfectly that ran through his mind.

He'd held her hand and thought that if he could show her how much his body wanted her, how desirable he found her, she could possibly see it in herself.

But her shying away from him both as he tried pushing up her skirt to eat her out in the greenroom, and then when he had her naked, kissing down her tummy to lick her for punishment, told him he hadn't done his job properly. And maybe he wouldn't be able to.

"How do you plan on helping?" Her voice held a hint of doubt but also hope.

"Come here." 성준 pulled her hand to follow him to the full-length mirror at the entryway of the hotel room. He felt her tug back, hesitating to stand in front of the mirror. He dropped her hand, not wanting her to feel forced to do anything she wasn't ready for, and stood naked and alone in front of the mirror.

"I like my abs," he stated, staring at his own naked frame reflecting back at him.

Beside him, he heard a small laugh followed by, "Of course you do. Who wouldn't?"

"But I don't like my chest." He touched his pecks where he always wished he could build more definition.

"I like my hands." He held up his hand. "But I wish my arms were stronger."

"성준, what are you doing?" Sophia finally did take a step closer to the mirror, which made his heart skip a hopeful beat. *That's not normal for a one-night stand.* They made a heart race from excitement and lust, not skip as if...

"I'm trying to show you that everyone is insecure about their bodies. But even with being insecure about it, I can still love myself. No one is perfect. No one will ever be perfect," he explained.

He watched her shuffle closer, and with a deep breath, stepped beside him, her eyes closed, but they slowly opened in the mirror. She hugged her stomach as she took in her nakedness. He caught her eyes scanning between his body and her own.

"I like my mouth." He continued his list as his eyes met hers in the mirror. "My tongue got to taste you." They both smiled at that. "But I wish my teeth could be straighter and whiter."

"성준..." She watched him in the mirror.

"I wish my dick was bigger, I wish my legs were stronger so I could be a stronger dancer. I wish——"

"I like my breasts." She cut him off.

"I do too." He smiled, moving to stand behind her, his hands coming from behind to grab her tits while their eyes remained on each other in the mirror.

"But I don't like my arms." She lifted her arm and gently shook. He watched it jiggle. He dropped her one breast and brought his hand to trace her arm up and down with his fingers. She shivered, and goosebumps raised on her arm. He said nothing; telling her that he liked her arms wouldn't change her opinion of them. But if he could give her shivers of pleasure in places she didn't find desirable, then maybe he could keep her mind off her insecurity and help her to focus on enjoying the feelings she was experiencing instead.

"I like my eyes." She smiled, causing her eyes that had been sparkling with tears to now glimmer with potential.

"Go on." He wasn't going to break eye contact. His hand squeezed her breast, and his other one traced her arm. She arched her ass back to push into his dick.

"I like my thighs. I wasn't too fond of them until…" She trailed off.

"Until?" he prompted, needing to hear the answer.

"Tonight." He saw a blush rise to her cheeks, and her body warmed, which sent a shiver down his spine. He pressed his dick harder into her ass.

"진짜?" His hand that had been playing with her arm moved down the side of her torso and down to her thighs, reaching between them to feel how wet she was.

Her head fell back with a gasp.

"성준," she moaned out his name.

"네, 자기야?" he whispered against the shell of her ear.

"Please," she begged.

"Please what?" His finger found her clit, and her head shot back up, her eyes meeting his in the mirror.

"Please…" she moaned out again.

"Tell me, Sophia," he demanded, pressing on the bud.

"Please fuck me," she finally blurted out.

"As you wish." He smirked. "Lean forward and put your hands on the sides of the mirror."

"What are you—"

"I'm doing as you begged. I'm going to fuck you. But I'm adding something I want. This is a mutually beneficial relationship, correct?" He grinned as she nodded vigorously. "You're going to watch me and tell me more things you like about yourself."

He walked away quickly to grab a condom and came back to see her bent over, hands on both sides of the mirror like instructed.

"Such a good little slut." He spanked her ass and watched as his handprint started to form. He ripped the wrapper with his teeth, grabbing the slippery rubber and sliding it down his cock. Spreading her cheeks, he saw her tight little hole, a hole he hoped he would get to enjoy at some point. There was somewhere he was aching to be first. He pushed his dick into her dripping pussy that was begging to be filled by him. She cried out as she took all of him. Every inch. er walls clenching around his cock.

It was heaven. 성준 had been to heaven and back in just one pump. He took a glance in the mirror to see her head down. He reached forward, grabbing the hair at the base of her neck and sliding upward to get a good grip, then pulled her head up.

Her mouth open, cheeks flush, her eyes hazy with lust as they met his in their reflections.

"Head up, 자기야. Watch yourself and tell me something else you like about yourself." He demanded as their eyes met and he pulled out of her. "For everything you tell me, you will get me inside you."

"I like…" He pulled her hair, seeing the smile that grew on her face as he did. "…my lips."

He pushed himself into her.

"My hair."

He pulled again as he gave her a few pumps for each thing she mentioned. He felt her walls clenching onto his cock so hard. She was already near her breaking point.

"More." He commanded, and he spanked her ass. She pressed harder into him.

"My ass," she all but screamed.

"That's it." He slapped her ass once again. "Keep going, 자기야."

He loved hearing the sounds of his pelvis slapping against her ass, the wetness as he pushed in and pulled out of her delicious cunt.

"I love my hips." As she said it, she rotated her hips to grind on his cock, and he could feel her walls squeezing around him. It made him twitch.

He took notice of how her wording had changed: "like" had turned to "love." He knew it wasn't totally possible that he could change her self-consciousness in one night, but he would fucking try his best.

He let go of her hair and put his hands on her hips, pulling her ass to him so her could pump harder into her.

"You're ready to cum aren't you?" he growled.

"네,네,네,"she screamed, letting him have all the control.

"Fuck, your cunt is so tight. I love it. I love it so fucking much. You're so beautiful, 자기야." He continued his brutal pace, her continuous clenching starting to make him lose control. "I need you to know how fucking gorgeous you are. I will let you cum when you realize how you take people's breath away."

"성-성—" She kept trying to say his name, but every hard pound into her caught her breath, and the words stuck in her throat.

"You can scream my name as you cum, 자기, but I need you to look at yourself in the mirror right now."

He watched her lust-drunk eyes try to focus. Her mouth hung open, and he could see her neck glistening from the heat they had created together in the room.

"Do you see yourself?" he asked, and she nodded, his hand still in her hair, still pulling. He continued with another round of questions. "Do you see everything you said you liked about yourself? What you said you *loved* about yourself?"

She again nodded, her eyes leaving her own reflection and finding his gaze, which was solely focused on her. He caught the satiated smile that was curving her lips.

"Say my name," he snarled. "Scream it as you cum."

"성준!" And just like that, her dam broke, squeezing his cock as her whole body shuddered. He continued to pump into her to make sure she enjoyed every moment of her high.

Once Sophia caught her breath, he pulled out of her earning a small whimper of disappointment.

"More," she whispered.

"응?" He wasn't sure he had heard her correctly.

"More. I want more." She was staring at him in the mirror.

I really don't think one night will be enough. That excitement in his heart was coming back.

"Come here." He pulled her shoulder to have her stand straight, but he could see her legs wobble. He turned her around to face him. Some hair clung to the sides of her face from perspiration.

He led the way over to the bed.

"Lay down, Sophia." He spoke softly, and like the good girl he knew she could be, she followed the command, laying on her back.

"Please, 성준," she begged.

He spread her legs wide, seeing the delicious mess she'd made dripping down her pussy. He was going to have that all over his face again. Maybe even another night if he could get it.

He put his cock at her entrance, still so slick from her release, and slowly pushed in, her hips bucking up to meet his. He reached behind her to grab the pillows from the head of the bed and put them under her hips.

"I love being inside you. You take my cock so well, Sophia." He smirked, leaning down, his hands hitting the mattress on either side of her head.

Her hands went to his chest and scratched down, prompting him to pump harder into her. They both moaned.

"You're so fucking beautiful," he said, dropping down to kiss her. Their mouths in a heated battle as the sensation at the base of his spine again told him he was going to cum.

He continued pumping hard into her, hearing the headboard hitting the wall, sending him to his boiling point. But just as he was about to let his release fill the condom, he remembered wanting to coat her chest in his cum.

He pulled out, ripped the condom off and used his hand to get the final few pumps to coat her chest and stomach. Euphoric didn't cover how alive his body felt as he watched his cum slowly drip down between her breasts. She was a mess. A stunning, breathtaking mess and it was all for him. He wanted it to only be for him. Could there be a way for her to be his? Was he genuinely considering pushing aside his idea of a different person at every stop?

His mind didn't give him time to think. 네! It shouted. *You want Sophia. No one else.*

Their heavy breaths mixed, and he moved to fall on the bed beside her. As they both caught their breath he sat up.

"Shit." He stood. "Let me get a towel."

"Wait." She reached up to grab his wrist.

They stared at each other for a few seconds, his eyes observing his cum dripping down her breasts and stomach, before she asked, "How about we shower together?"

With the happiest grin on his face, he responded, "Fuck yes."

KOREAN VOCABULARY:
진짜 – jinjja – really

CHAPTER ELEVEN

Sophia braced her hands against the tile of the shower, the water cascading onto her back and falling around her breasts and stomach as 성준 spread her ass cheeks apart and, with precision and determination, pounded into her puckered hole. She loved the pain that was building her pleasure.

One of his hands left her ass and reached around her waist, his chest pressing against her back as his fingers landed on her clit. With a few more pumps into her, they both reached their climaxes. As she moaned out his name, his teeth marked her once more. She wanted all the marks he made to last forever. She never wanted to forget this night with him.

He slowly pulled out of her ass, her knees going weak, but she leaned more heavily against the shower wall and tentatively stood straight. The hot water soothed some of her aches as his arms wrapped around her waist, like he knew what she needed. He was such an attentive lover. She would miss such care.

"Guess we should actually clean up now," he whispered with a deep chuckle before kissing the shell of her ear. "We need to rest a bit if we're going to make this night last."

Sophia shivered imagining all the deliciously depraved things they still had yet to try in that hotel room, and then she quivered as his hands moved from her waist. He grabbed the shower gel and began massaging her shoulders like an expert, moving down her back, her moaning getting louder.

"This makes you moan almost as loud as my dick does." 성준 laughed, continuing down her back, over her ass, and down her legs.

She slowly turned around, not sure how well her legs would keep her standing, but she wanted to see his face. A face she'd only imagined she could see through a screen or on a stage. A face she still couldn't believe was so close to her own.

"My turn." She smiled as his hands moved back up, that immaculate face of his meeting hers and his lips gently pressing against hers.

"I'm all yours." He smirked, giving her one more kiss before stepping back, allowing her to have full access to him.

She loved his body. Never in a million years did she think she would have that kind of access to him, every inch of him. What fan thought they could? But she made it a point to be present in this moment; she was going to enjoy all the time she had with him.

Sophia lathered up her hands with the floral-smelling soap and began to run them over his chest. Those firm pecks he thought needed to be bigger, she enjoyed just the way they were. His arms that he wanted to be stronger, she was thrilled could lift her up.

She realized 성준 had been right about how people thought of their bodies. Where she might've found flaws, others could find beauty. Which meant she should find the beauty in herself as well. Their mirror escapade was already a large step in her loving her body and her own journey, and possibly even his.

"고마워." She smiled softly, her hands stilling on his lower abdomen.

"뭐가?" He raised an inquisitive brow.

"You've made me realize something I think I somewhat knew but kept buried and hidden." She dropped her hands from his waist and smiled. "You're right that most people point out their flaws. Even in the things we like about ourselves."

"Oh?" His smile held a sad understanding as he took a step

closer to her, the water washing off the lather on his chest, his hands moving to grab her hips.

"I need to love the fact that I'm not perfect. And something I find imperfect, someone else could find perfect," she choked out as a tear fell that she hoped he wouldn't notice and would think was just a water droplet from the showerhead.

But 성준's hand cupped her cheek and wiped away the tear. He blinked rapidly, which made her wonder if he was possibly crying as well. He leaned forward, and she closed her eyes, thinking he was going in for a kiss, but instead she heard a squeak, and the water stopped.

"Let's dry off," he murmured, and her eyes popped open.

He was quiet as he climbed out of the shower. Something was different. Sophia wondered what she'd said that could've made his demeanor change so drastically so quickly. He grabbed towels and walked over to wrap one as best he could around her body. But hotel towels were a tiny excuse for a bath towel. She ended up just using it to dry her hair.

"여기서 기다려." He walked out of the bathroom and came back with bathrobes. He held one open for her to slip into, and once on, he came to the front to tie it before he put on his own.

He grabbed her hand and walked them out of the bathroom and brought them to the bed. Sitting, he gently pulled her hand to have her sit beside him. With every second of silence, her worry grew.

"성준…" She trailed off, unsure of what to say.

"너 그럴 자격 있어." He spoke as he squeezed her hand in his.

"네?" She turned to face him better.

"You deserve to love yourself, Sophia." He cupped her cheek again. "You *deserve* it."

She wasn't expecting that response, but it caused her heart to pound so hard in her chest, she was scared she would never be able to feel how she was feeling in that moment ever again.

"You deserve that as well, 성준." She reached out to cup his cheek too. "You have those hundreds of thousands of CLARvoyants who love you. But you also need to feel that about yourself. You've showed me that. That's why I thanked you."

"Fuck, Sophia." His voice was strained. She caught that his eyes *were* blinking back tears. He was just as insecure as any other person. And why wouldn't he have those same feelings? The truth was, he was an everyday person, just with a fancy job title.

"We both deserve it. Let's both love ourselves." She grinned and leaned over to kiss him.

"Yes, let's." He smiled against her mouth before claiming her lips once more and gently pulling them down onto the bed.

Korean Vocabulary:

고마워 – gomawo   thank you

뭐가? – mwoga? – for what?

여기서 기다려 – yeogiseo gidalyeo – wait here

너 그럴 자격 있어 – neo geuleol jagyeog iss-eo – you deserve it

CHAPTER TWELVE

There was a bright light assaulting Sophia's eyes, and when she blinked, she realized she had fallen asleep. After their shower, where more mind-blowing orgasms rocked both their bodies, they had a few more orgasms around the room before climbing into bed to rest. She thought she had only closed her eyes for a few minutes, but apparently it was a few hours.

Did she ruin his plan to go all night? Was he annoyed that she fell asleep?

A panic set in that she had overstayed her welcome and 성준 would want her out before he woke up.

She sat up quickly to begin the silent search for her belongings but was surprised to see 성준 sitting in the desk chair, a piece of furniture he had bent her over the night before, with a cup of coffee in one had and his phone in the other.

"잘 잤어?" He smiled, getting up from the chair and walking over to kiss her on the forehead. The sweetness was unexpected, and she happily accepted.

"네." She responded by wiping the sleep from her eyes, but she also rubbed them to make sure it wasn't a dream.

"I wasn't sure what you would want to eat this morning, so I ordered just about everything they had on the menu." He walked toward the end of the bed, where several carts of room service sat.

"You didn't need to do that." She blushed at how sweet he was being after how much he commanded and dominated her throughout the entire room the night before.

"I didn't, you're right." He handed her a robe. "I wanted to."

She reached to grab the robe and felt how sore her body had grown as the high of her many, many, *many* orgasms wore off. She let out a groan and his face filled with concern.

"Don't worry, 성준, I'm fine." She eased. "I haven't done anything like…" They both blushed before she cleared her throat to continue, "…like that, honestly ever."

They laughed together.

"Me neither. The first time I ever asked a woman, she told me I was a freak and no one would be into that. After that I thought maybe I was weird." He sat down beside her on the bed.

"You're not weird. Well, I mean, maybe a bit weird considering you mentioned eating 소떡소떡 while I was blowing you." She laughed and his echoed.

She enjoyed seeing the unrestrained joy on his face. His eyes crinkled and his lips parted, his mouth wide, flaunting his perfect teeth, and his face turned a light shade of red. She hadn't seen a laugh like that from him since before CLAR1T officially debuted. She had watched all their vlogs and behind the scenes, and she could count on her hand how many times she had seen a laugh as bright and happy as she was witnessing firsthand.

"I meant to ask why you said that?" she asked after their laughs settled.

"미안. That's a code the boys and I use." He wiped a small tear from his eye and continued, "Each of us has our own food that we say we're going out to get. That way, if our manager is looking for us or if someone hears our conversation, they don't question it."

"Oh wow… So you guys are rule breakers?" Sophia smiled in amusement at learning a new fact she could assume not many people knew about. A secret she would keep forever.

"Not often, but for important things, yeah." He smiled and grabbed her hands, which she had turned into robe paws with the sleeves.

"Getting laid is a *very* important thing," she joked as she released her hands from their paws to hold his big ones.

"The *most* important." Leaning forward, he kissed her softly. He pulled away, and she had every intention of grabbing the back of his head to keep kissing him because something as simple as his kiss made her wet and hungry for more.

"The boys will be here in an hour," he said as if he could read her mind about wanting more. Or maybe he also wanted some morning sex before she had to leave. He grabbed his phone to look at the time, and she realized it wasn't an invitation to have more sex, it was a countdown for her having to leave.

"어." She pulled the blankets off her to climb out of bed and search for her clothes.

"뭐 해?" he asked.

"I'll make sure to be out of here in the next twenty minutes. They'll never know I was here. I promise." She picked up her skirt and pulled it up, under the robe.

"야,야,야." He grabbed her wrist to stop her from throwing her nightmare hair up into a messy bun. "I was just letting you know when they would be here so you could pick the food you wanted before they come. They'll devour all these plates before you can blink."

"You mean you want me to stay?" She wasn't sure if her jaw had dropped to the floor or not, but it felt like it was there.

"Why do you sound so surprised?" He pulled her onto his lap.

"One-night stands don't usually spend more than that time together. But also, meeting your groupmates…" She hadn't expected him to want her to meet his groupmates. A group she had just been fangirling about only eight-ish hours ago.

"I'm sure they're curious about what kept me away the whole night, and tonight if you're interested." He slipped a hand between her thighs.

"Tonight?"

"We're here for one more night before going to the next stop," he explained as he pressed for her to spread her legs to let him slip even higher up. "I would also like to spend some more time with you. That is, if you would also like that."

"Are you kidding?" She stood to turn and straddle him.

"Do you not want to?" He frowned.

"That's not what I meant." She cupped his cheek, feeling the cheesiest, widest smile grow on her face. "I just thought you would want to maybe meet someone else."

"I was shocked I met you. Really surprised." He grabbed the hand holding his cheek. "You were the first person to see my message and follow through with giving the sign. And when I saw you, I was blown away."

"Message?" She didn't know what he meant until he brought his hand between them and showed two fingers pointed downward. It finally clicked. The tweet. "Oh my God. That tweet? That was you?"

He nodded with a small chuckle. "I've had that account for years. I never posted on it. It was my small escape during some of the stressful moments during training and debut. The company never found out about it. I thought that while on tour I could use it for my own *needs*. I decided to finally use it and made that one post you saw, but no one ever reacted to the message, and I didn't think anyone saw it until I saw you making the sign."

"I might've been your only option, but I'm glad you chose me." She dropped her head, embarrassed.

"I wasn't joking when I said I was blown away by your beauty. I was hopeful you would say yes to spending the night with me," he explained as his hands ran up her thighs to grab her ass and pull her farther onto his lap. His hardening cock pressing close to her core.

"And I want more nights. Maybe even more mornings as well." His smile was nervous.

"What about afternoons?" she joked, getting the sense he was asking for more than he was saying. And it was making her heart race, but she wanted to be sure she understood.

"Afternoons could also be included—when I'm not filming our

tour vlogs, that is." He squeezed her ass and leaned up to kiss her neck.

"성준, are you asking for this to be something more?" She dropped her head back to allow him more access to her neck, where he'd already made several marks the night before.

"I am," he responded quickly.

She pulled her whole body back, her head snapping up so her eyes could meet his. He was serious.

"If you think I'm asking you just for the sex, you're wrong." He moved to place her next to him instead of straddling him, and she was still surprised at how he lifted her as if she was as light as a feather. "When we were in the shower and were talking, and even in bed as you were falling asleep, you were mumbling about your life and even started admitting how much you love CLAR1T and how much we had changed your life." He laughed and his ears turned red as her own cheeks flared.

"I didn't mean to fangirl after sex." She covered her face.

His hand grabbed hers and brought it to his lap.

"That wasn't it." He shook his head. "I loved how free you were, how open about yourself you could be. You weren't trying to be someone else. I haven't had that kind of relationship, minus my groupmates, in several years. I hadn't realized how someone else being so free and acting only as themselves could allow me to be myself. And after you fell asleep, I watched you for a second and thought I wanted you…" His eyes met hers, making her nervously excited to hear what he was going to say. "…to be mine."

If her hands weren't being held by 성준, she would've tried to pinch herself to be one thousand percent positive she wasn't in a dream.

"You don't have to give me an answer right now." He brought his hands to his lips, pressing gently, "Pick the breakfast you want. The boys will be here soon."

She'd had no clue the previous night would happen, and she definitely didn't think 성준 would be asking for any kind of relationship. She needed to think about what he was offering.

"Are there waffles?"

. . .

KOREAN VOCABULARY:
잘 잤어? – jal jass-eo? – Did you sleep well?

CHAPTER THIRTEEN

Sophia had just had breakfast with CLAR1T. She was still unsure the night before had happened, but then the other five members of the group came to 성준's room, and he happily introduced her to all of them. She was nervous and speechless at first, but then they began to ask her questions about herself, and she even got to ask them questions that she, as a fan, wanted to know. She found that just like 성준, they were normal everyday people who just happened to be famous. They soon had to leave for the press and to get ready for the concert that night, so they all left, allowing her alone time again with 성준.

He asked for her to wait an hour or so to make sure everyone from the crew was gone so she could make a clean getaway. He even gave her a quick peck before leaving her, but his eyes hinted that he wished she had given him an answer to his proposal.

After Sophia left the hotel, she had a lot to think about. Not only did she have the most intense orgasms of her life all night with an idol she had pictured as just another celebrity eight hours ago, but he had asked to meet with her again that night, and suggested that they keep it going even after.

He had felt something between them. Something she had also

felt. But her mind fought her, questioning if they had both been caught up in the moment and a real relationship wouldn't work out. How could it? He lived across the globe, he traveled the world on tour, he was a *freaking K-pop idol*! Meanwhile she was still trying to figure out what she wanted to do with her life.

She needed an outside party to weigh in on the matter. And she knew just the person.

Sophia made her way to her part of town and walked right into her bestie's coffee shop to throw a "hypothetical" problem at Bridgette to help her solve.

"Sorry we're not open ye—" Bridgette's beautiful wavy strawberry-blonde hair swayed in its ponytail as her head popped out of the kitchen behind the counter, but upon seeing Sophia, stopped mid-sentence, came fully out of the kitchen, and gave Sophia a once-over. "That's the outfit you wore to the concert…"

Sophia looked down, not thinking about how her outfit would be a dead giveaway that her hypothetical was going to be so obviously not hypothetical.

"Where the hell have you been? And with who?!" Bridgette walked out from behind the counter and right up to Sophia with the brightest, most excited smile.

"A coffee and croffle first. Then I will explain." Sophia started pulling down chairs from their resting places on their tables to help Bridgette while also trying to avoid more immediate questioning.

"So you hooked up with one of CLAR1T's staff last night, and it was the best you ever had. He asked to meet you again tonight and hinted at wanting more and you…said what?" Bridgette took the last sip of her coffee after she wrapped up what Sophia had told her.

She had lied about *who* she had slept with to keep 성준's privacy while laying out what happened. She knew what could happen if word got out. Not that she didn't trust Bridgette, but better to keep them both safe.

"Wasn't able to give an answer and kinda basically ran back here." Sophia grabbed the empty plates and coffee mugs and brought them to the back sink in the kitchen.

"You like him, right?" Bridgette shouted from the front.

"Of course I do." Sophia responded by returning to drop back into the seat across from her best friend.

"Besides the sex?" Bridgette raised an eyebrow.

"That's such a ridiculous question!" Sophia got defensive.

"Is it?" Bridgette bit back.

"Yes! Because of course it was more than the sex," Sophia snapped back. "We had moments of vulnerability where we talked about things we were scared of, but also what we were hopeful for. It sounds crazy, but I felt the most open with him in that eight-hour span than I have even with you in our years of friendship."

Bridgette smirked but then feigned shock. And while it caused them both to laugh, it was also like a slap in the face to Sophia. Why had she stalled to answer 성준? What had she been afraid about?

Sophia knew in that moment she needed to give him a proper response. She grabbed her phone to send a text to him about meeting up after his concert, but the screen stayed black. Dead.

"I need to borrow your phone charger." Sophia waved her phone.

"You need to go home to your apartment next door, charge your phone, and shower the sex smell off you so you don't scare away my first few morning customers of the day." Bridgette shooed Sophia to the door.

"It's not that bad!" Sophia rolled her eyes with a laugh.

"Girl, besides the sex glow you have the sex smell. Get out of here!" Bridgette chuckled as she pushed Sophia out the door.

———

AFTER CLIMBING OUT OF THE NICE HOT SHOWER THAT HELPED SOME of her muscles relax, and getting all her thoughts in order on what she was going to say to 성준, she sped to her charging phone. When she saw it light up, having enough charge for her to

swipe up to her home screen, she noticed she had an email notif-
ication.

While she wanted to ignore it and focus on what she had
planned to say to 성준, something told her to open the email.
Pressing the icon, it opened to a familiar email address and the
subject stating something about her teaching job in Korea
application.

Holy shit.

CHAPTER FOURTEEN

성 준 had wanted Sophia to stay, but she told him she had to go home and change before she met up with her friend to talk about the concert because her friend hadn't been able to go due to work.

She had said she wouldn't tell her friend about what happened, as she didn't want to compromise his privacy, but to him it was confirmation she wasn't going to accept his proposition of something more. He wasted no time after she left to delete not just the tweet but the whole Twitter account. For him, it was only Sophia.

When did I become such a lovesick puppy?

Had he been stupid for asking? They only knew each other for a night. And a lot of the night was him fucking her in every and any position he had dreamed about.

The boys had met her that morning, and while she was nervous at first around them, once she saw how they were just normal guys, he watched a bond building.

He knew starting a relationship would be hard. He was an idol first, himself second. But Sophia made him want to focus on being himself some more.

"You really like her, don't you?" Woo Shin said as they sat around the greenroom before the night's show.

"뭐?" 성준 asked, coming out of the daydream he was having.

"We've never met a woman you've involved yourself with," he nudged to the rest of the group, who were getting their hair and makeup done. "Not that you had a lot, but I can tell you like Sophia more than anyone before. Enough to have us meet her."

"I do," 성준 admitted. There was no use hiding it with his groupmates. They were the brothers he never had. They were his family. "Fuck, I really do. Last night was like nothing I've ever experienced before. She let me do things I only ever thought about. And not just that, she is smart, strong, and breathtakingly stunning. She's—"

"You got it bad." Woo Shin chuckled. "Did you mention all of this to her?"

성준 nodded. "I think I scared her away when I asked to see her again."

"She has your number, right?" Woo Shin asked. 성준 again gave him a nod. "She'll call. I saw the way she looked at you—"

"That's because I'm in her favorite group."

"She didn't look at any of us the way she did you," Woo Shin argued, but 성준 wasn't convinced.

With a loud huff Woo Shin continued, "그러니까… We see fans fall over themselves to be near us all the time. You should be able to spot the difference. Think about it a little bit longer."

"When did you become such a romantic?" 성준 laughed. Woo Shin raised his hand to mimic that he was going to hit 성준.

"I've always been, you just have never been in love for me to share romantic advice with." Woo Shin raised his hand back.

"Let's go, boys!" Minhwa jumped to get the rest of the group pumped up about the show starting soon.

성준 WAS EXHAUSTED FROM ANOTHER AMAZING SHOW. THE CROWD was alive, which made him want to perform his heart out. But when he grabbed his phone before the meet and greet only to see no message from Sophia, he felt defeated. He wiped sweat off his face as the fans began to funnel into the meet and greet, and he waved and held hands with all of them. Fake smile and laugh at the ready for every person who walked past him, while internally his heart had a little crack in it.

He just wanted it to be over. His mind was filled with thoughts of Sophia. And only Sophia. The faces that walked past were blank; they weren't Sophia's. He waved. He gave finger hearts. But as his mind was shutting down from the monotony, something caught him by surprise.

An upside-down V.

He almost threw it back but froze. Shooting up from his chair, his eyes trailed up the arm. It was covered by a leather jacket, but once up the arm he saw a familiar neck. *His* bite marking *his* woman.

"Sophia," he whispered. The rest of the group turned to look as well.

She smiled and waved before she walked down to the rest of the boys. He had to get his mind together. But his bandmates were ahead of him. They threw the downward V, and security intervened, grabbing Sophia by the arm and pulling her out of the line.

She smirked, gave 성준 a wink, and then her entire demeanor changed. Her expression turned frightened, and she started begging the security guard to let her go. The rest of the fans started to whisper among themselves, which meant her little scene worked.

When the last person finally left the room, 성준 ran down the hall to the greenroom where he knew she would be held.

Swinging open the door, he saw her standing in the middle of the room. She had taken off the jacket to reveal a distressed shirt that had rips hinting at the skin beneath. He couldn't help but yearn for the breasts underneath that he'd had his face buried in the night before, and hoped to have buried in again. Dark jeans hugged her hips and waist. A waist he wanted to grab onto, hips he wanted to grind against him as she rode his cock.

"Sophia," he breathed out in relief to see she was, in fact, real.

"As a true CLARvoyant, I *had* to buy tickets to both shows in my town." She laughed as she shuffled her feet.

He smiled but wasted no time, closing the door as well as the space between them. He grabbed the back of her head and pulled her lips to his.

"성준," she mumbled against his lips.

"If I only get this one last night with you"—he kissed down her jaw and her neck, finding the spot he had marked the night before—"I'm not wasting time with small talk."

He tangled her hair in his hand and pulled so she exposed more of her throat.

"I don't want this to be the last night," she moaned, which made him pause his exploration of her neck to get a good look at her face.

"You're saying…" He needed her to be crystal clear.

"After I left this morning, I thought about what you said. All day it played on repeat in my mind." She smiled and cupped his cheek. "I thought about how much I enjoyed my time with you. Not just the sex, which was—"

"Amazing. The best I've ever had." He kissed her softly.

She giggled but pulled back to finish what she had to say.

"Yes, it was all of those things, but it wasn't just the sex. Like you said, when we talked in front of the mirror, and in the shower when we helped wash one another, and as we fell asleep and you told me about how you struggled to adjust to being an idol, I knew that you trusted me as much as I trusted you."

She shook her head, dropping it down to hide her face. He didn't want her to be nervous or scared. He wanted her to know how happy he was.

"Sophia, I do trust you. And I really like you. I know being together will be hard. Not only the distance, but the secrecy. But that will only be for the next year and a half." He spoke quickly.

"A year and a half?" she asked.

"That's what's left in our dating clause of the contract."

"No, I meant, you think you're going to want to keep seeing me in a year and a half?" Her smile grew slowly across her face.

"I can't see into the future, but as strongly as I have fallen in a

day, I have a feeling a year and a half is only the start of our story."
성준 smiled and kissed Sophia sweetly.

He dropped her hand, wrapping his hands around her waist, pulling her against him.

"I guess I should mention distance won't be as big of an issue as you think." She smiled between his pecks.

"어?" He raised a quizzical brow.

"I applied for a teaching position in Korea. When I left this morning, I heard from the school." She paused. "I won't be in Seoul, but a short train ride away," she explained. "I know how cliché that sounds, an American teaching English in—"

He cut her off with a searing kiss, silencing her immediately. He bent down, his hand landing just under her ass, and lifted her to spin them around in excitement.

"성준, put me down!" She softly punched his shoulders. "I don't want to hurt—"

He pinched her ass and slammed her up against the wall, his body pressing against hers. "If you finish that sentence I'm going to punish you until you won't be able to sit or walk, and I will *have* to carry you everywhere."

"약속?" she chided, biting her lip.

"Sophia…" His voice dropped, and he felt her shudder. Now he knew another thing she liked. He trailed a finger down her neck and wrapped his hand around her throat. "So, you interested in fucking an idol for a while?"

KOREAN VOCABULARY:

그러니까 – geuleonikka – therefore

약속? – yagsok? – promise?

EPILOGUE

A *year and a half later…*
성준 pulled on the levers of the swing to hit that sweet spot he knew would make Sophia scream and send him over the edge as well. The swing was one of her best apartment additions.

"Fuck yes, 자기야. Scream like the dirty whore you are." And with that, she screamed his name, her walls caved around him, and he gave those final good pumps to let them both ride out their highs.

When they started to breathe at a somewhat normal pace again, he helped her out of the swing and carried her to the bed, laying beside her, tracing her waist and hips with his fingers as her hand roamed his chest.

"Do you know what today is?" he asked, kissing her forehead and tasting the saltiness of her sweat.

"June 6?" She scrunched her face, most likely wondering why he had asked such a question after their sex swing fun.

"Yes," he laughed, "but it's also a rather important date."

She leaned forward to kiss him. "Well, tell me!"

He rolled over to grab his phone off the bedside table and unlocked it to open his Instagram feed. His heart was hammering in his chest. He had been working toward this moment for the last few months.

"I talked to some people at my company. And after a lot of back and forth, they agreed to do what people are calling 'soft launching,'" he started, and he watched her eyes go wide as she sat up straight. He liked watching her tits bounce, and he was hard again.

He needed to tell her everything before he was inside her again.

"I know what a soft launch is, but your contract——"

"The clause ends today. As of…" He looked at the time. "One minute ago. All of CLAR1T are free to date."

He hit the icon to post a picture on Instagram and then turned it toward Sophia. Her eyes widened even more, if it was possible. She grabbed his phone and began swiping. He knew she was analyzing the photos. Photos he had taken in secret of them together. None showing her face, keeping her all to himself. He wanted to keep her private life private to an extent. But he also wanted the world to know he had someone he was obnoxiously in love with.

While she continued to scroll, he leaned down to his small travel bag he always brought to visit her and waited for her to get to the last photo.

"서-성-성준," she stuttered. "이거 뭐야?"

She turned the phone back to him, and he opened the velvet box to reveal the very same pair of simple twisted-vine white gold rings nestled in velvet.

"Promise rings." He nervously pulled one from its place and turned it toward her. "I've hated having to keep this a secret. Sophia, 사랑해. And I want everyone to know. But I also know I want you safe, so I shared you without sharing you. To tell the world how desperately I am in love while keeping you anonymous."

She put her hand out to let him slide the ring on, then she grabbed the other ring from the box and snatched up his hand to slide it on his ring finger. She leaned down to kiss the ring.

"성준, 사랑해. You were such a surprise in my life, and I can't believe you're the man I'm in love with. All because I trusted a stupid fucking tweet." She laughed as tears fell from her eyes.

"I have never been happier that I posted a stupid fucking tweet."
He laughed, his eyes filling with tears as well. He leaned forward to
kiss her and finished, "I was captivated by you the second I saw you.
I had no clue that night would change my entire life. You're the
most beautiful woman. You're strong, intelligent, kind, powerful,
loving, a freak in bed," he joked, making them both chuckle even as
tears fell down their faces. "You laugh at my bad jokes, your smile
enraptures me, your heart is pure… Fuck, I could go on for eternity
about all the ways I love you."

He always told her how much he loved her, but now it was out
to his hundreds of thousands of followers and fans.

"I want to spend forever telling you all the ways I love you, if
you'll let me." He smiled nervously.

"성준, you will always have me. Hell, I extended my work visa
just to stay closer to you, knowing I wouldn't be able to stay away
for too long. You make me feel magical. I love watching you become
the man I fantasized about and even more." She kissed him. "I'm
ready to stay for as long as you'll have me."

"Fuck." He pulled her closer to him. "I want you forever, 자기
야."

"Then forever it is." She wrapped her arms around his neck,
straddling him, and he felt her core against his hard cock.

With a devious smile on both their lips he asked, "Ready to *love*
an idol for forever?"

KOREAN VOCABULARY:
사랑해 – saranghae – I love you

ACKNOWLEDGMENTS

We have reached this moment again. Once again, I am in awe of the fact you made it here. And the fact I made it here as well. There are always countless people to thank but once again the first credit always goes to the love of my life and father of our (soon to be) child. The only man who ever could make me change my mind about having a kid in the first place. Hahaha.

The second always goes to my parents. My mom for keeping me in this crazy game of the writing world and the one I can bounce ideas off of. And my dad for always being a happy shocked when I tell him how many books I sold in a month.

Third credit goes to all the people who make this whole self-publishing thing a little easier for me. My BETA readers who had me giggling at their reactions to scenes and appreciating their input on helping the story more exciting for other readers. My amazing editor Christie from Proof Positive. My magnificent formatter Garnet Christie. And last but definitely not least, the girl who brings the characters to life on the stunning covers she has created Kim Cavrak.

Fourth is to everyone who is still in this with me for the long haul. I have never and most likely will never be able to put into words just how much your support, your words of encouragement, your love for the characters I've created, and your unlimited kindness has meant to me over these last few years and for the many years to come. Let's keep this going eh!?!

WANT CLARiT MERCH?

https://ko-fi.com/koreanfromcontext/shop

WANT TO STAY UP TO DATE WITH SAMANTHA ANN?

Website: www.koreanfromcontext.com
TikTok: @koreanfromcontext
Instagram: @koreanfromcontext
Threads: @koreanfromcontext
X/Twitter: @koreanfrmcntxt
Buy Me A Kofi: https://ko-fi.com/koreanfromcontext

READ MORE BY SAMANTHA ANN

Seoul Searching
Matching Set
An Afternoon in Monaco (short story on Ko-fi)

The Idolized Series
HER ULT

Non Korean Works
Traveler (Romantasy on Vella)

CONTINUE YOUR KOREAN EDUCATION

Teuida
Papago
DeepL
Viki (Learn Mode: On)
Netflix (Language Reactor Plug-in)
Lingo Legend

NOTES